MILLIONAIRE DAD:
WIFE NEEDED

MILLIONAIRE DAD: WIFE NEEDED

BY

NATASHA OAKLEY

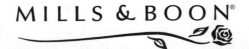

MILLS & BOON®

First published in Great Britain 2006
Large Print edition 2006
Harlequin Mills & Boon Limited,
Eton House, 18-24 Paradise Road,
Richmond, Surrey TW9 1SR

© Natasha Oakley 2006

ISBN-13: 978 0 263 18997 1
ISBN-10:   0 263 18997 X

Set in Times Roman 16½ on 19¼ pt.
16-0806-49707

Printed and bound in Great Britain
by Antony Rowe Ltd, Chippenham, Wiltshire

CHAPTER ONE

THERE was no one there.

Lydia Stanford set her heavy briefcase down and banged again on the dark blue front door of the cottage, stepping back to look at the top floor windows that peeked sleepily out of a roof of handmade tiles.

It was picturesque, but she wasn't here to admire the view and it all looked ominously quiet. There was no glint of movement in the upstairs rooms. No sound of radio or television in the background. Nothing.

Well, nothing except the half-open window above the ramshackle single brick addition at the back. She lifted the brass plate covering the letterbox and peered inside. 'Ms Bennington? Are you there?'

Total silence.

'Ms Bennington? It's Lydia Stanford. We have an appointment at ten.'

Had an appointment at ten, she corrected silently. It was now nearly twenty past. *Damn and blast the woman.* Where was she? Lydia straightened and shook back her hair. *What exactly was she supposed to do now?*

Was it possible Wendy Bennington had forgotten their meeting? Lydia wrinkled her nose and stared at the closed door as though it held all the answers. It didn't seem likely she'd have forgotten. The woman was in her late seventies but had a mind so sharp she made politicians quake at the knees the minute she opened her mouth. She'd lay money on her not forgetting a thing. Ever.

Which was why she'd grabbed at the chance to write an authorised biography of Wendy Bennington. It was the kind of *once-in-a-lifetime* opportunity which meant she'd broken off her first holiday in five years. Why she'd got the first flight back to London and had immersed herself in researching the inveterate campaigner's astonishing life.

So where was she? Lydia peered round the empty garden as though she expected to see

Wendy Bennington walk up the path. Just yesterday the older woman had sounded so enthusiastic about the project; surely she wouldn't have gone out? And leaving a window open? No one did that any more.

Lydia sucked in her breath and considered her options. She could, of course, get back in her car and drive back up the motorway to London. Or she could go and get a coffee in Cambridge and come back in an hour or so. Either one would be an irritating waste of her time.

She pushed the bell and rattled the letterbox. Even though it didn't seem worth doing, she bent down and shouted loudly, 'Ms Bennington?' Through the narrow opening she could see the green swirly patterned carpet, but nothing else. The cottage seemed completely deserted.

She half closed the plate, her fingers still on the brass. It wasn't a voice or even a definite noise that made her pause. Perhaps it was a sixth sense that something was wrong. She called again, 'Ms Bennington, are you there?'

Silence. And then a soft thud. Almost.

'Hello? Hello, Ms Bennington?'

She couldn't be absolutely certain, but she thought she heard the sound again. Not a footstep or someone falling...nothing that obvious. But something. She was almost sure of it.

Lydia straightened and shifted her briefcase into her other hand. Of course it could be nothing more exciting than a cat knocking over a waste-paper basket, but...

But if that soft noise had been the elderly lady's attempt to attract attention she wouldn't thank her for walking away and leaving her. Would she? She'd expect her to use her initiative...and do something. Which meant...

What?

Lydia chewed gently at the side of her mouth. It had to be worth a try at getting into the cottage through the open window. If Wendy Bennington had been taken ill...

It *was* possible. She might have fallen. Accidents in the home were very common, after all. If anything like that *had* happened, trying to get into the cottage would be the right thing to do. She glanced down at her watch, now showing twenty-five minutes past the hour.

With sudden energy, Lydia quickly walked round to the back of the cottage and stared at the small upstairs window. It was tantalisingly open. If she could just climb on to the flat roof, reaching the window would be child's play. It didn't look that difficult.

She glanced over her shoulder. There was no one around. No one to ask if they'd seen Wendy Bennington that morning.

There was no choice…

Lydia carefully concealed her briefcase beneath a large rhododendron and stood back to consider her options. It really wasn't going to be difficult—as long as the flat roof was strong enough to take her weight.

She took a moment to pull a black velvet scrunchie from her jacket pocket and twist her long hair into an untidy topknot before pulling the dustbin up against the wall. Then, holding on to the drain pipe, she hoisted herself up the first few feet—just high enough to get a grip on the roof.

Easy. Well, perhaps, not easy…but easy enough. And if Wendy Bennington wasn't home it would be just as straightforward getting out again. No one need know.

With the dexterity of the county-level gymnast she'd once been, Lydia swung her leg up and pulled herself on to the roof. If nothing else she could tell the elderly woman her home was a security disaster. Anyone could break in. Where she lived in London no one would dream of doing anything as foolish as going out and leaving a window open. You didn't even leave your car unattended in Hammersmith for five minutes without careful thought.

'What the hell do you think you're doing?'

A man's voice shot through the silence. Lydia's hand paused on the open window, her heart somewhere in the vicinity of her throat.

'Get down! Now.'

Startled, she turned and looked at the man standing below on the crazy paving. Tall. Handsome…in a scruffy, rough kind of a way. Mid-thirties, maybe late. It was difficult to tell.

And angry. Definitely angry. No doubt about that at all.

'What the hell do you think you're doing?' he repeated.

Lydia moved away from the open window. 'Getting in. I thought I heard a noise.'

'Really?'

'Yes, really,' she fired back, irritated by the heavy sarcasm in his voice. How many burglars did he know who went out on a job dressed in a genuine Anastasia Wilson jacket? It was time he took a reality check. 'I had an appointment with Wendy Bennington at ten—'

'It didn't occur to you to wait until she answered the door?' he asked with dangerous politeness, his accent at odds with his very casual clothes. Lydia looked at him more carefully. Whoever he was, he certainly wasn't the farm labourer she'd thought he might be.

And he wasn't as handsome, either. He had a hard face and an arrogant stance that made her want to explain the principles of feminism— very slowly—because he'd probably never grasped the concept of equality.

'It occurred to me, yes—'

'So, what changed your mind?' he asked, still in that same supercilious tone of voice.

Lydia struggled to hang on to her temper. 'Forty minutes standing about in the garden is probably what did it. I'm going to climb in and see if she's hurt. If that's all right with you?' she added, turning her back on him.

'It isn't.'

She looked round. 'Pardon?'

'I said, it isn't.'

'Don't be so…stupid. I had a ten o'clock appointment. I'm sure Wendy wouldn't have forgotten, it was too important. She might be lying hurt inside. Have you thought of that?' Lydia turned and pushed the tiny window open.

'I'd rather you used the key.'

'What?' She swung round in time to see him open the back door. 'H-How did you do that? The door was locked. I checked—'

'She keeps a spare key under the pot.'

Lydia watched him disappear inside with a sense of disbelief. *Damn it!* This couldn't be happening to her. It had been a very long time since anyone had managed to make her feel so completely foolish.

Logically she knew there was no reason for her to have known Wendy Bennington kept a key hidden. The idea that a formidable campaigner of human rights would keep her back door key under a terracotta flowerpot seemed, frankly, incongruous. But clearly she did…and the local populace all knew about it.

At least this particular member of it did. Who in…blazes was he anyway? *Arrogant, sarcastic, supercilious…* The words flowed easily. It didn't help knowing she might have reacted in a very similar way herself if she'd discovered someone about to break into a neighbour's upstairs window. Presumably he *was* a neighbour?

Gingerly Lydia lowered herself down, careful not to scrape her jacket on the brickwork. She brushed herself down and picked up her briefcase from under the rhododendron.

'Tall, dark and sarcastic' had left the door open, no doubt expecting her to follow him. She wiped her feet on the worn doormat and let her eyes adjust to the gloom. The small cottage window ensured the kitchen would always be dark, but the situation was made so much worse by the heavy net curtain hung on plastic-coated wire.

Lydia let out a low whistle. Even though the outside of the cottage was looking frayed around the edges and the garden was hopelessly overgrown, she honestly hadn't believed anyone lived like this any more.

The kitchen looked like something out of a nineteen-forties movie. There were no fitted kitchen units at all. Just a freestanding gas cooker that looked as if it ought to be consigned to a museum and a thickly painted cupboard with bakelite handles. The orange and cream marmoleum floor tiles had begun to lift and the whole room was dominated by a floor-standing boiler.

It was, frankly, grim.

She hadn't been aware that she'd had any pre-conceptions about what she'd expected Wendy Bennington's home to be like—but, clearly, she'd had many. She stepped over the twin bowls of water and cat food respectively and tried to ignore the faint odour of animal and stale cigarettes.

This had been a mistake. She should have stayed in Vienna, marvelled at the Stephansdom, eaten *sachertorte* and enjoyed the opera like any other sensible person. What the heck was she doing here?

She'd given up her holiday…for this. Crazy. She was crazy.

And there was still no sign of Wendy Bennington. The house was completely quiet except for the ticking of a clock somewhere in the further recesses of the cottage. She placed her briefcase down by the rusting boiler and looked across at the man as he flicked through the mail on the kitchen table.

'I'm Lydia Stanford,' she said with pointed emphasis, waiting for him to look up and acknowledge she was there.

'I know.'

'You know?' He said nothing. 'And you are?'

'Nick.' His eyes were still on the sheaf of letters in his hand. 'Nick Regan.'

Which told her absolutely nothing.

'Do you live nearby?' If he'd looked up he'd have seen her head indicate the direction of the only other house within a mile or so of the cottage. 'No.'

No? 'You're not a neighbour?'

He looked up at that. Very briefly. The expression in his brown eyes made it absolutely clear he'd no intention of assuaging her curiosity. 'No.'

Nick Regan.

Had she read his name anywhere in connection to Wendy Bennington? She was fairly sure she hadn't. All those hours on the Internet? All those pages of notes? Was it possible she'd missed something vital?

His accent spoke of an expensive private school education and his assurance indicated he was very used to being in the cottage. Comfortable, even.

Her eyes took in the expensive watch on his wrist and the soft leather of his shoes. Her mother had always sworn you could tell everything about a man by looking at his shoes. If she was right, this one had a bank account to be proud of, despite the worn jeans and faded jumper.

So who was he?

Someone Wendy Bennington had hidden from the public spotlight for over thirty years? A secret son?

She half smiled and pushed the thought aside. It didn't seem likely—which was such a shame because it would have made a great story.

It didn't fit, though. From all she'd learnt of Wendy Bennington so far, she'd have been more likely to announce it proudly. Her whole life had been characterised by a complete disregard for social conventions, so the absence of the 'father' wouldn't have deterred her. She'd have told the world that her son's father was an 'irrelevance' and no more than a biological necessity.

'Should your name mean something to me?'

He looked up and then back at the letters in his hand. 'No.'

Lydia frowned, irritated. What was the matter with the man? This kind of information was hardly highly classified. His behaviour was bizarre, to say the least. And rude.

'How do you know Wendy Bennington?' she persisted, moving closer.

He threw the pile of letters back on the kitchen table. 'I've known her all my life.'

'Really? How's that?'

His dark eyes flicked momentarily across to her and then he walked out of the room.

Lydia let out her breath in one long stream and just about managed to bite down on the expletive which was on the tip of her tongue. Perhaps he hadn't fully understood that *she* was the one with the appointment.

Pausing only to shut the back door, she followed him out into the narrow hallway.

'Wendy?' Nick Regan opened the door immediately to his left and glanced inside.

'Is she there?'

He brushed past her. 'I'll check upstairs.'

Lydia gave in to temptation and swore softly as he took the stairs a couple of steps at a time. Even allowing for the possibility that he was genuinely worried, there was really no excuse for his attitude towards her. Much more of it and he was going to get the sharp edge of her tongue.

Her hand was on the newel post as he shouted down to her, 'Get an ambulance.'

Ambulance?

'Quickly.'

Dear God. No.

Despite everything, she hadn't really expected that. For all her dramatic attempt at breaking and entering, she hadn't anticipated anything other than the elderly woman had popped out to get some milk.

Her mind played havoc as she pictured Wendy Bennington lying bleeding...or dead, even... She reached into her handbag and fumbled for her mobile phone while she ran up the short flight of stairs. 'What's happened?'

In the doorway she saw a figure, instantly recognisable despite the flamboyant caftan and grey flowing hair, slumped in the doorway. It wasn't the way she'd imagined she'd meet Wendy Bennington.

Every picture she'd ever seen had shown Ms Bennington to be a highly capable and formidable woman. Her energy and strength had radiated from each and every image. This woman looked simply old. Her face was filled with fear and complete bewilderment.

Lydia flicked open her mobile and glanced across at Nick, for the first time grateful she hadn't made this discovery alone. Presumably he would know whether Wendy Bennington was prone to bouts like this and whether she was on any kind of medication.

'I think she may have had some kind of stroke,' he said quietly, his long fingers smoothing back a lock of grey hair. 'Wendy?'

Lydia watched as the woman on the floor frowned and struggled to articulate what she was feeling—but what came out of her mouth was incomprehensible. Her words were slurred and her frustration mounted as she realised she was communicating nothing.

'Wendy, can you touch your nose for me?' Nick asked.

Again that frown, two deep indentations in the centre of her forehead, and yet there was no discernible movement. Nick looked over his shoulder. 'Have you rung?'

Lydia tapped out the emergency number and

waited for the operator's voice. It was only a matter of seconds, but it seemed an age before there was an answer. Her hand gripped on to the mobile until her knuckles glowed white and she forced her mind to stay in the present.

The last time she'd telephoned for an ambulance it had been for Izzy. Lydia felt her eyes smart with the effort of holding back the emotion those images unleashed. She'd never been so frightened as she'd been then. Waiting for the ambulance to arrive had been the longest fifteen minutes of her life.

It had seemed like every minute, every moment, had been stretched out to maximum tension and it was etched on her memory. The feeling of complete helplessness. The guilt. The regret. The panic. And the mind-numbing fear. A whole hotchpotch of feelings she hadn't even begun to unpack yet. All there. All reaching out towards her like fog in a nightmare.

But this was different, she reminded herself. The circumstances were completely different. She forced her breathing to slow and tried to focus on the questions she was being asked.

Nick looked over his shoulder. 'Tell them to take the left hand fork at the top of the lane. It's a confusing junction. They could lose five minutes or more if they take the wrong turn.'

Lydia gave a nod of acknowledgement and reached into her jacket pocket for the piece of paper on which she'd written the directions to the cottage. Wendy had been very thorough.

She watched Nick disappear into one of the bedrooms and return with a pillow and satin eiderdown. He used the pillow as a cushion and wrapped the elderly woman gently in the apricot-coloured eiderdown.

'Yes, the last cottage on the right.' The voice on the other end was precise and calming. 'About half a mile out of the village. Yes. Thank you.' Lydia finished the call and clicked her mobile shut.

'Well?' Nick turned to look at her.

'An ambulance is on its way.'

'Is there anything I need to do while I wait?'

Lydia shook her head. 'You've already done it. She said not to move her and to wrap her in something warm as she might be in shock.'

He smiled grimly and settled himself back down on the floor, taking Wendy's hand between his own. 'It won't be long now.'

Lydia watched the shadow pass across the elderly woman's face as she struggled to speak. She seemed so confused. Frightened. So unlike anything she'd been expecting to find in such a formidable woman—and yet would anyone be otherwise?

Her knowledge of strokes was woefully scanty, but she knew the consequences of them could be devastating. It didn't seem right. A woman of Wendy's courage couldn't be struck down like this. It wasn't fair.

But life wasn't fair, was it? It wasn't fair that her parents had died when they were so young. Or that her sister Izzy had miscarried her baby. Life had a way of kicking up all kinds of unpleasant surprises. She ought to know that by now.

Lydia put her phone back in her handbag, taking more care than usual to fasten the stud. 'Do you want me to put together an overnight bag? Or s-something…?' Her voice faltered as he looked up, his expression conveying exactly what he thought of her suggestion.

'I'll do it later,' Nick said curtly, 'and take it when I go to the hospital.'

What was his problem? He looked as though she'd told him she'd ransack the entire room instead of offering to gather together a few toiletries and a nightdress. Her eyes shifted to Wendy's hugely swollen ankle, visible beneath the eiderdown. 'I'll get some ice.'

'Sorry?'

'For her ankle. Whether it's broken or just sprained, ice will help it.'

He followed the line of her gaze. 'Right.'

Lydia turned and started down the stairs before she thought to ask, 'Does she have a freezer?'

'In the old scullery. She keeps a chest freezer out there.'

Lydia continued down the stairs. As she reached the bottom she jumped as a warm furry shape twisted round her legs. 'Hello,' she said softly. The cat mewed loudly and pushed that little bit closer. Lydia stooped and ran her hand across the sleek black fur.

Stepping to one side, Lydia carried on to the kitchen. Two concrete steps led down to the old scullery, the ancient copper wash tub in one corner. The freezer stood, large and white, on the far wall. Spots of rust discoloured the surface and the lid seemed to have slightly bowed.

There was so much about Wendy Bennington's house that made her feel unutterably sad. It was as though the elderly woman did no more than camp here. She'd certainly made no effort to make the place feel comfortable…or even like a home.

The freezer was in desperate need of being defrosted and Lydia struggled to lift the lid. She chipped off huge chunks of ice and lifted out the top basket.

Inside there were countless boxes of pre-prepared meals for one, half-opened packets of stir-fry and frozen vegetables. Surely more than enough to feed a single person for several months? Lydia lifted out a small packet of peas and headed back upstairs.

Nick turned as soon as she got there. 'Have you found something? Her ankle seems to be bothering her now.'

'You'll need to wrap this in a towel. It's very cold.'

But even as she spoke he'd pulled out a pillow from its pillowcase and tucked the frozen packet inside. She watched as he carefully held it up against the swelling and heard Wendy's small moan of pain.

'Is there anything else I can do? I'd like to help.'

Nick glanced up. 'If you want to be useful you could take your car down to the village and point the ambulance in the right direction.'

'I'm sure there's no need for that. I found my way here without a problem.'

'But it's a single track road and if they miss the junction there's nowhere to turn for a couple of miles.'

Lydia frowned, uncertain what to do. What he was saying about the junction was true—but it was more than that. He so clearly wanted her to leave.

She heard the elderly woman mumble incomprehensibly and wondered whether he wished her to go because he knew how much Wendy would hate being seen this way. If the situation was reversed, if she were the woman lying on the floor, she would prefer there were no strangers to see it.

And there was no doubt that Wendy trusted Nick implicitly, not once had she glanced across in Lydia's direction. Her eyes searched out his as though they would be her salvation.

It felt intensely private. His strong hand calmly held Wendy's frail agitated one in his. Lydia didn't think she'd ever seen a man so gentle or so eminently capable of managing a situation alone.

'I'll wait in the village.'

Nick scarcely noticed she'd spoken; his mind and energy were focused entirely on Wendy Bennington.

As it should be, she reminded herself. Of course, he should be totally concerned about the sick woman.

Lydia reached inside an inner pocket of her handbag and pulled out a business card. 'Would you call me? I'd like to know how Ms Bennington is doing.'

He turned, his expression unreadable. If he wasn't a poker player, he ought to be. She couldn't tell whether he thought it reasonable that she wanted to know what happened to Wendy or whether he thought it an intrusion.

'Please?'

His face didn't change, but after a short pause he reached out and took her card. 'Make sure you leave the front door open,' he said, tucking it in the back pocket of his jeans.

Lydia supposed she had to take that as an agreement that he would call her. Whether he would remember to actually do it or not was a different matter.

Quietly she walked down the stairs and into the oppressively gloomy kitchen. Her briefcase was still by the rusting boiler where she'd left it. Lydia bent and picked it up, before taking a last opportunity to glance about her.

Sad. It was a truly sad place.

Slowly she walked along the hall and carefully put the front door on the latch. It was strange that Nick Regan let Wendy Bennington live in such a way. He so obviously loved her. It was in the way he'd brushed her hair off her forehead and held her hand.

So who was he? Why was he *so* concerned about Wendy Bennington? It surely went beyond being a mere friend, but his name hadn't appeared in her research. As far as she'd been able to ascertain, Wendy had no family at all. Not even a nephew. An only child of only children.

She walked down the narrow front path, mulling over the possibilities. At the gate she stopped, mouth open in disbelief. His car was parked immediately in front of her own—and her mother's wealth barometer had been spot on. Nick Regan drove a top of the range sports car. *So who the heck was he?*

Lydia opened her car door, feeling vaguely ashamed. There was something in her which made it impossible to switch off 'the journalist'. Why couldn't she merely be pleased that Wendy had someone who loved her? Wendy had lived her life entirely for other people; it was right that when she needed help herself there should be someone to give it. Someone who cared because they chose to, rather than doing so out of a sense of duty.

She tipped the front seat of her more modest car forward and slid in her briefcase. Perhaps she hadn't been so far adrift in thinking he was behaving like a son? *It had to be a possibility because what else was there?*

The engine purred into life and Lydia took a last glance back at the cottage through her rear-view mirror. He was the right kind of age. Thirty-four, maybe as much as thirty-eight. Certainly no more.

Perhaps he was the result of a passionate affair? She let her imagination soar. An affair with a married man? Or the husband of a friend? Or was he a sperm donor baby? Or…

She was getting ridiculous. If Wendy Bennington had ever been pregnant someone somewhere would have written about it. She glanced up again at her driver's mirror and groaned at the image she presented. Her hair was still bunched up in a childish topknot. Hardly the look of an award-winning journalist. *Damn.*

She ripped out the scrunchie and let her hair fall softly around her shoulders. Nick bloody Regan probably thought she was some kind of tea girl rather than the woman his…friend…had chosen as her biographer.

It shouldn't matter. Lydia crunched her car into first gear. It *didn't* matter—at all. But…but this was not turning out to be a good day.

Nick heard her leave. First her footsteps on the stairs and then the sound of her car pulling away. He let out his breath in a steady stream and tried to settle himself into a more comfortable position on the floor.

He hadn't expected Lydia Stanford would give up so easily. Her kind always stayed to the last. They circled overhead, waiting for the kill, like the scavengers they were. The wonder was that she hadn't whipped out her camera and taken some photographs as 'background colour'—or whatever she called it to salve her conscience.

Nick rested his head against the wall. There were other journalists, with far better credentials than Ms Stanford, who would have been more than anxious to write an authorised biography. Some he would have trusted to do a fair and balanced job of it.

But Lydia Stanford…

No. He wouldn't trust her as far as he could spit. What Wendy had been thinking of to insist on a woman capable of building her career by using her own sister's tragedy he couldn't imagine. You had to be an automaton to do what Lydia had done.

Any normal person would have been overcome by grief at her sister's attempted suicide. They'd have hung by her bedside, too traumatised to do anything else.

But not Lydia Stanford. Ms Stanford had launched an exhaustive vendetta against the man at the centre of the scandal. She'd meticulously collected information on his fraudulent business dealings, making sure she had enough to ruin him.

And in the process she'd made her own fortune. Not bad going. *But what about the sister?* How did she feel about being a stepping stone in her sister's career?

Even his ex-wife, Ana, wouldn't have been so coldly calculating. He rubbed a hand across the spike of pain in his forehead. *Or just not as overt?* But that made precious little difference to the people around them. They still got hurt. Collateral damage in a game they didn't know they were playing.

One thing was certain; Wendy's decision to choose Lydia Stanford had nothing to do with the mane of honey-brown hair which she wore in that half up, half down sexy thing women did. Nor would Wendy have noticed the amber flecks in her brown eyes, or her long legs, or, he altered his position slightly, her unfortunate taste for his ex-wife's jacket design. Presumably Ms Stanford thought it worth selling her soul to be able to afford an Anastasia Wilson jacket. Now Ana would most certainly have approved of that.

Nick shifted uncomfortably on the floor, listening out for the sound of the ambulance. He stroked the hand in his lap. 'It can't be much longer, Wendy. Hang on in there for me.'

He watched the frown of concentration and heard the quietly determined, 'Apple.'

He leant closer. 'What about an apple?'

With total concentration she carefully repeated, 'Apple.'

It made no sense. Nick kept stroking her hand and tried to sound calm and reassuring. The minutes ticked by interminably slowly.

He tried to picture Lydia Stanford at that crucial junction making sure the ambulance crew didn't waste precious minutes. She'd do that, he decided. She might have ambition running through her veins where lesser mortals had blood, but he believed she'd take a few moments to help the woman whose biography she'd agreed to write.

Even Ana would have spared a few minutes from her hectic schedule. His smile twisted. Or perhaps not. Ana spared no thought for anyone but herself.

The garden gate banged and he sat a little straighter. *Thank God.* 'Up here,' he shouted.

He heard the mumble of voices as they came into the hall; seconds later a face appeared at the top of the stairs. 'Wendy Bennington, is it?' the woman said, taking in the slumped figure on the floor.

Nick nodded, standing up and brushing down his jeans.

'Your friend made sure we didn't miss the turning.' She knelt down and spoke to Wendy. 'I'm Sarah. We'll soon have you sorted, my love.'

CHAPTER TWO

IZZY put a plate of spicy crab cakes and salad in front of her sister. 'So, tell me. What's the matter?' She sat down opposite Lydia and flicked back her softly waving hair. 'I might have overdone the chilli in the dipping sauce, so go careful.'

Lydia took a mouthful of the crab cake. 'This is fantastic.'

'I know. It's the Tobasco.'

'You're getting good.'

'I'm a genius,' Izzy said, smiling over the top of her glass of wine, 'but that's not why you're here, is it? What's happened?'

'You mean apart from Wendy Bennington having a stroke?'

Izzy nodded. 'Apart from that. Although it's horrible for her, of course. I don't mean it isn't, but...'

The silence hung between them.

'You've seen far worse things than an elderly woman having a stroke, Liddy.'

Which was true.

'So, what's bothering you?'

Lydia sighed and looked across at her younger sister, uncertain as to what it was that was nagging at her. It seemed to be a whole mixture of things twirling about in her head making her feel discontented. Irritated. That wasn't the right word either.

It was as though she'd been travelling happily in one direction only to have it violently blocked off. Like a train being derailed, if you liked. Normally she'd have worked out a way to make it an opportunity, but…

Lydia winced. It didn't feel like an opportunity. It felt—

She didn't know what it felt like. There was something about seeing Wendy Bennington slumped in that doorway that had affected her deeply—and in a way she found difficult to understand. Instead of driving back to Hammersmith she'd rung Izzy and begged a bed for the night.

But why? Her sister was absolutely right when she said she'd seen and experienced so much worse.

In her nine years as a journalist she'd witnessed many terrible things. Not just death and injury, but mindless violence and examples of sadistic cruelty that defied description. Some days it was difficult to maintain any kind of belief in the innate goodness of human nature, but she'd trained herself to cope with it. She was inured against it all.

Almost.

Certainly detached. Lydia picked up her wineglass and sipped. It was as if a steel screen came down and kept her objective. It was the only way it was possible to do her job. She imagined it was similar to the way a surgeon worked. You could care, really deeply, but not so much that it prevented you from thinking clearly.

She looked across at Izzy, patiently waiting, her hands cradled around her wineglass. The only time in her life when she'd felt completely out of control was when she'd found Izzy unconscious. There would never, could never, be any event more terrible than finding her sister had taken an overdose.

She hadn't felt detached then. That night she'd experienced emotions she hadn't known she was capable of feeling. She'd believed Izzy would die and fear had ripped through her like lightning in a night sky. There'd been the sense of being utterly alone and desperately frightened. Not even the unexpected death of her parents had inspired such an extreme reaction.

The only thing that had kept her functioning, on any level, was the passionate hatred she felt for Steven Daly—the man responsible. Bitter anger had uncurled like a serpent within her. It had driven her. Had demanded retribution.

Looking at Izzy now, little more than two years on, it could almost have been a dream. She looked so young—and hopeful. Time was a great healer.

'Well?' Izzy prompted.

Lydia forced a smile. 'I think it was the house,' she said at last, trying to put words on thoughts she couldn't quite catch hold of. 'You've never seen anything like it. She lives in a cottage that time's all but forgotten. All alone in the middle of nowhere.'

'Perhaps she likes solitude? Some people do.'

'It's not that… It's…' Lydia frowned. 'The cottage smells of damp and cat urine…and then there are all these frozen meals for one in the freezer. It's so incredibly…sad. There's no other word for it—' She broke off. 'Oh, no!'

'What?'

'I'd forgotten about the cat.' Lydia put down her wineglass. 'She's got a cat.'

'It's not your problem, Liddy.'

'But who's going to feed it?'

'Probably the irritating Nick Regan. It really isn't your problem,' Izzy repeated, taking in her sister's expression. 'If not him, there'll be a neighbour.'

'You think?'

'There's bound to be.'

Lydia relaxed. *Of course there was.* Wendy Bennington went abroad for long stretches of time. There were bound to be structures in place to take care of her pet. Lydia picked up her knife and fork. 'You're right. I know you're right. It's just…'

Izzy smiled. 'You really like this Wendy Bennington, don't you?'

'I hardly know her.' Lydia cut a bite-sized piece off her crab cake. 'We've spoken on the phone half a dozen times, no more. I'd never met her face to face.' Until today—when she'd been confused and frightened. Nothing like the woman she'd been expecting. The image of her slumped in her bedroom doorway hovered at the front of Lydia's mind.

'But you like her. I can tell you do.'

Lydia paused, fork halfway to her mouth. *Did that explain it?* She certainly admired Wendy. Had been flattered and very excited at the prospect of writing her biography.

Izzy seemed to follow her thoughts. 'There's no reason to think you won't still write the biography. Give it a few days and see how serious her stroke was. You might be surprised.'

'I might,' she conceded.

'Perhaps that Nick Regan will phone you.'

Lydia pulled a face. 'I'd be surprised at that. He didn't like me at all.'

'Why?'

'No idea.' Lydia thought for a moment. 'It didn't help that he found me standing on a flat roof, trying to get into the cottage through an upstairs window, but—' she looked up as Izzy gave a sudden spurt of laughter '—I don't think it was that.'

'I can't think why. Most people would think it odd.'

Lydia shook her head, a reluctant twinkle in her eyes. 'It probably didn't help,' she conceded, cutting another mouthful off her crab cake, 'but he *really* didn't like me. At all. You know, eyes across a crowded room, instantaneous dislike. No mistaking it.'

'Is he handsome?' Izzy sat back.

'That's irrelevant.'

'It's never irrelevant.'

Lydia ignored her.

'Well, is he?'

'No.' Even without looking up she could feel Izzy smile. She put down her fork. 'Not exactly.'

'Which means he is.'

'It does not!'

And then Izzy laughed again. 'He is, though. I searched for his name on the Internet while you were having your shower. He's gorgeous. A bit like…what's the name of that actor in… Oh, stuff it, I can't remember. Regency thing. You used to have him as your screensaver.'

'The actor from *Pride and Prejudice?* Nick Regan looks nothing like him!' Lydia protested.

'Not exactly, but a bit. He's got the same brooding, intense expression. At least, this Nick Regan does. He's an inventor. I think.' She waved her hand as though it didn't matter in the slightest. 'Basically, he *is* Drakes, if you get what I mean. He owns the company and came up with the idea of the electrical component in the first place. Worth millions.'

Lydia frowned. 'He can't be. That's Nicolas…' *Regan-Phillips.* She closed her eyes. *Damn it!* It couldn't be.

Could it? And, if so, what *had* he got to do with Wendy Bennington?

'I've bookmarked it for you to see.'

'I'll look later.'

Could Nick Regan be Nicolas Regan-

Phillips? Izzy must have made a mistake. A multimillionaire corporate businessman and a human rights campaigner—what could possibly link the two together?

The cottage had been securely locked up. Lydia moved the terracotta pot with very little expectation of finding the key beneath it—but there it was.

She clutched the small tin of cat food and bent to pick up the key. If the almighty Nicolas Regan-Phillips had anticipated she might return to the cottage he might not have put it back there. So much for his apparently awesome ability to read character, but at least the cat wouldn't starve.

The back door opened easily. Izzy had laughed at her for deciding on making the thirty minute detour, but it felt like the right thing to do. How could she return to London knowing she could have done something to help Wendy but had chosen not to? And this was little enough.

'Cat,' she called softly. She set her handbag on

the stainless steel draining board. 'Cat, where are you? Breakfast time.'

The bowl of leftover cat food on the floor looked revolting. Lydia picked it up with two fingers and carried it across to a plastic swing-bin. 'Why do people keep pets?' she mumbled softly to herself, turning back to the sink and giving the bowl a swill out. 'This is disgusting.'

'To keep them company?'

Lydia gave a startled cry and whipped round.

'Because they love them?' Nicolas Regan-Phillips said, leaning against the kitchen doorway, looking much more like the photograph Izzy had found than he had the day before. He wore a sharp and very conventional pinstripe suit. Power dressing at its most effective.

And he *was* handsome. Her sister's words popped into her mind and she silently cursed her. The resemblance to her favorite actor was really very superficial, but it was there all the same.

'I—I came to feed the cat.' Lydia turned away and pulled back the loop on the tin, irritated at the slight nervous stutter. *Where had that come from?* And, more importantly, why?

'So did I.' He placed a brown paper bag down on the draining board.

'I hope you don't mind that I—' She stopped herself, swinging round to look up at him as a new thought occurred to her. 'How did you get in?'

He held up a key. 'Front door.'

'Oh.' Lydia cursed herself for the inanity of her reply. Of course he would have Wendy's key. He would have needed it to lock up the cottage. What was the matter with her?

She carefully scooped out the contents of the tin with a spoon, aware that Nick continued to watch her. He made her feel uncomfortable, as though, perhaps, she'd been caught out doing something he considered wrong rather than the good deed she'd intended. 'I suddenly remembered I'd seen a cat. I couldn't leave it to starve,' she said, glancing up.

He really did have the most inscrutable face. Normally she was good at picking up emotional nuances—but Nicholas Regan-Phillips seemed to short circuit some connection and she was left uncertain.

On balance he didn't seem as angry as he'd been yesterday. More suspicious. She looked away. It probably wasn't anything personal. He had a reputation for avoiding journalists and for protecting his privacy. Lydia swilled out the empty tin under the tap. 'Does Wendy have a recycling bin?'

'I imagine so.'

Lydia looked up in time to catch his swift frown. If she puzzled him she was glad. He certainly puzzled her. What had he to do with Wendy Bennington? She hadn't managed to discover any connection at all. It was a mystery—and mysteries really bugged her.

'Shall I leave this on the side then?'

'I'm sure that'll be fine.'

Lydia carefully placed the tin at the back of the draining board and rinsed the spoon. 'How's Wendy?'

There was a small beat of silence while, it seemed, he evaluated her right to ask the question. 'Better than she looked yesterday.'

Lydia glanced over her shoulder, a question in her eyes.

'She's had a TIA. A mini-stroke, if you like. She'll be fine.' His mouth quirked into a half-smile. It was a nice mouth, firm and sensual. 'No permanent damage, but she's been told to make some life changes.'

'That's…fantastic.'

His smile broadened and something inside her flickered in recognition. 'I'd love to hear you try and convince her of that.'

'When will she be home?'

'Well—' he stretched out the word '—that depends on who you speak to. She's broken her ankle. It's a fairly simple break, apparently, and doesn't need surgery, but…'

Lydia looked around her and then down at the uneven floor levels.

Nick followed her gaze. 'Exactly. She's not going to manage here for a few weeks, however much she'd rather be in her own home.'

'No,' Lydia agreed. She placed the clean bowl back on the floor and picked up the other one. 'So, who's won?'

'The cards are stacked in my favour. I'm here to pick up Nimrod. Hopefully lure him in with food.'

Lydia emptied the water into the sink and put in some fresh. 'That's the cat?'

'Nimrod, the mighty hunter,' Nick agreed, moving away into the hall, his voice slightly muffled. 'I gather his namesake was Noah's great-grandson.' He reappeared moments later, carrying a cat basket.

'Great name,' she said, smiling at the incongruous sight of a city gent with rustic cat basket.

'Certainly appropriate. He's something of a killer cat. Wendy picked him up as a stray a couple of years ago, only he turned out not to be so much a waif as a con artist. If it moves, Nimrod will hunt it. There never was a cat more suited to life in the wild.'

Lydia laughed. 'Good luck getting it into that thing then,' she said with a gesture at the cat basket.

'So Wendy's warned me,' he said, setting it down on the kitchen table.

She rinsed her hands under the tap. 'I'm glad it's all sorted. It suddenly occurred to me, after I'd left, that you might forget about…Nimrod. I was going to contact you today.'

'How?'

She looked up, surprised by the abrupt single word question. 'It wouldn't have been too difficult. A call to your company…'

His nod was almost imperceptible, but she could see his attitude towards her change. 'I thought you didn't know who I was.'

'I didn't, but you have an Internet presence—'

'And you checked.'

Lydia thought of Izzy and smiled, deciding that she wouldn't tell him that her description of him had inspired her sister with a burning fascination to discover who had managed to rile her so much. There'd been little enough information to find, nothing he could object to.

He was thirty-six and divorced. His only child, a daughter, lived with her mother and he was hugely successful at what he did. Nothing particularly unusual in any of that.

'Do you always pry into other people's business?'

'Pretty much.' She looked about her for a towel on which to dry her hands. 'It's an occupational hazard. But, this time, you've got to acknowledge I was invited to pry.'

'Not by me.'

'By Wendy.' She turned to face him. 'Though I dispute the use of the word pry.'

His eyes narrowed. 'Do you?'

'She's led an amazing life. Don't you think it's in the public interest to have that properly chronicled? What she's achieved, particularly for women, is amazing.'

'I think what's deemed to be "in the public interest" is stretched beyond belief,' he said dryly, 'but that's not to undermine what Wendy has achieved.'

'Can't argue with that, I suppose—but I'm not here as a representative of any tabloid paper. Wendy will have complete control over what I write about her and, as long as it's truthful, I've no problem with that.'

'No?'

'Absolutely not.'

She sounded aghast, but Nick knew better. Confronting Lydia Stanford was like coming up against a snake in the grass. You could never trust her. Never.

Very early in her career she'd worked undercover to highlight the ill treatment of the elderly in care homes and, while you couldn't question the validity of her findings…you had to be suspicious of her ability to lie. And lie convincingly enough for colleagues to trust her.

Wendy might be impressed by her ability to stick to her purpose, of owning a cause and staying with it, whatever the personal cost—but he suspected a different motivation lay at the heart of it. He suspected her only cause was herself—Lydia Stanford. And where was the virtue in that?

She carefully folded the towel and threaded it back through the loop. 'So how do you know Wendy?'

'You don't give up, do you?'

Lydia smiled, her eyes the colour of topaz. Warm and beguiling. 'It's usually easier to give in and tell me what I want to know.'

He turned away as though that would stop him being drawn in. 'She's my godmother.'

'Really?'

'I have the rattle to prove it.'

She laughed. It was the kind of laugh that

made him wish she was a different woman—
and they were in a different situation. He ran
an irritated hand through his hair. *He'd been
celibate for far too long.* That rich throaty
chuckle was exactly what could make him
forget who and what she was.

'Actually, that's a lie. She didn't give me a
rattle. I received two engraved napkin rings and
a boxed china bowl and plate set from the other
two.'

'And from Wendy?'

'A copy of the Bible, the Koran and the
complete works of William Shakespeare.'

He watched the way her eyes crinkled into
laughter. She was dangerous. You could easily
relax in her company, forget that she used
anyone and everyone near her to further her career—even a vulnerable sister.

People often described him as ruthless, but he
would never have taken something so intensely
personal and used it to advance his career. Lydia
Stanford might claim that her sister had made a
complete recovery, but he doubted it.

Betrayal was painful—acutely painful—and

when it came so close to home it was difficult to ever recover from it. He had personal experience of it and her Anastasia Wilson jacket was a visual reminder.

Better to remember how that betrayal had felt. Better to remember how much pain the woman who'd decreed that jacket should be in precisely that caramel colour had inflicted. It didn't matter that it exactly picked out a shade in Lydia Stanford's long hair. Or that it accentuated a narrow waist and visually lengthened her legs.

It was a warning. And only a fool would ignore it.

'Have you read them?'

'What?' He brought Lydia back into focus. Her lips parted into a smile, showing her even teeth. The woman was stunning. Like a sleek lioness. A mixture of sunshine and fire.

'Have you read them all yet? The Bible, the Koran and the complete works of Shakespeare?'

'By the age of thirty-two.'

'I'm impressed.'

'I've never used the napkin rings, though,' he returned and was rewarded by the same sexy laugh. Hell, it did something to his insides that didn't bear thinking about.

He closed his hand round the handle of the cat basket. 'Have you seen Nimrod?'

'Not yet, but I'm sure he'll come in for food some time. He can't have had anything to eat since yesterday morning.'

Nick glanced down at his wristwatch. 'He'll have to do it in the next twenty minutes or I'll be out of time.' He strode over to the back door and called.

'Do cats come when you call?'

He looked over his shoulder. 'No idea.' Lydia was smiling, bright eyes ready to laugh and, God help him, he wanted to laugh back.

'Look, why don't you let me try and catch Nimrod? I can stay until he comes in for food.'

'I couldn't ask you to do that. I—'

'Why ever not?' She shook back her hair. 'You're obviously busy and I'm on holiday.'

'On holiday?'

Her smile twisted. 'I should be in Vienna. I flew back when I heard Wendy wanted me to write her biography.'

'You broke off your holiday?' He couldn't quite believe it. What a pointless gesture. His godmother would have been more than happy to wait. There was nothing so important about the precise timing of this meeting which meant it couldn't have been postponed.

'Guilty as charged. Over-developed work ethic.' She smiled, but this time it didn't have the same effect. Nick could see a different face.

It was none of his business whether or not Lydia Stanford chose to curtail her holiday, but it reminded him of Ana. Still, four years after she'd left, he thought about her most days. There were reasons for that, of course. Good reasons.

In the three years they'd been married Ana had never taken a holiday. Had never turned off her cellphone. It was a price she'd been prepared to pay to achieve her goals. He couldn't deny she'd been totally honest about that from the very beginning, and at the start he'd admired her for it.

Presumably Lydia Stanford would agree that that kind of commitment was necessary. They were wrong.

'I've got the laptop in the car. I can work here and drive Nimrod over to you later.' She looked across at him. 'It's not a problem.'

Nick glanced down at his watch. It was tempting to accept her offer. He had back-to-back meetings scheduled for the morning and paperwork that really needed looking at after that, besides squeezing in a visit to the hospital. But to accept meant…

She seemed to read his mind. 'Don't worry. I shan't take it as an endorsement of your god-mother's choice of biographer.' She met his eyes. 'By the way, what is your problem with me?'

'Have I said there's a problem?' he countered.

'You haven't needed to. It's obvious.'

He hesitated. 'Wendy is capable of making her own decisions. In fact, she would strongly resent my interference in what doesn't concern me.'

Even in his own head his reply sounded pompous and formal. Famed for his 'tell it like it is' approach to business, how had he become so verbally challenged when confronted by a beautiful…?

What was she? Not a blonde or a brunette.
Richer than a blonde and lighter than a brunette.

'I don't believe that for a minute.'

He looked up.

'Oh, I believe Wendy doesn't like interference in her business. I'm like that myself,
but—' her eyes met his '—but I don't believe
you don't tell her what you think. I've seen you
two together, remember.'

He felt a small muscle pulse in his cheek. 'I
don't want her hurt.'

'I won't.'

And, strangely, he believed her. There was an
innate honesty in those rich eyes that made him
want to trust her. Was that how she worked? Was
it a highly cultivated technique which persuaded
the unsuspecting to share their innermost
secrets?

'If you slander her in any way I'll sue you.'

She didn't flinch. 'An authorised biography is
just that—authorised.' Then her face softened.
'You really love her, don't you?'

'She's a special lady.'

'So I gather.' Lydia slipped her arms out of her

jacket and placed it over the chair by the table. 'You can trust me. Where do you want me to take Nimrod to? Do you have a housekeeper to receive him?'

A housekeeper. A nanny. A daughter.

He didn't trust her. Not with one atom of his body. If he left Lydia in the cottage she would, no doubt, look around. She'd open drawers and search through Wendy's possessions. But then, Wendy herself had argued that she'd nothing to hide.

Let her search.

'My housekeeper is Mrs Pearman. Christine Pearman.' It felt as if he'd lost some unspoken battle. 'Did your research on me extend to knowing where I live?'

As soon as the words left his mouth he regretted his phrasing of them. Lydia Stanford was doing him a favour. Even if she did have an unacknowledged agenda of her own.

'You weren't that much of an interest, but I'm sure I can find out with a couple of phone calls if you want to make it a game.'

He'd deserved that, Nick thought as he fished

in his pocket and pulled out his card case. 'It's a ten, fifteen minute drive from here. No more.' He scribbled down the address. 'I'll ring Christine and let her know to expect you. You'll need to phone up to the house when you arrive and they'll open the gates.'

Lydia took the card and looked down at it.

'If you need to leave before Nimrod puts in an appearance, I'd be grateful if you'd leave a message with my secretary and I'll come back this evening. The number's on the front. It's a direct line through to her. I don't want you to feel you have to sit here for hours.'

She turned the card over. 'It's not a problem.'

'No, well…thank you.'

Her eyes flashed up. 'You're welcome.'

'I'll lock the front door. If you leave the key beneath the flowerpot…'

'No problem,' she said again.

There was nothing left to do. 'The cage is here.' He pointed at the cat basket.

'Yes.'

It was just leaving that was the problem. It was walking back down the hall and shutting the door.

Trust. This was about trust. About leaving her alone in Wendy's cottage.

Or was it? There was the suspicion that this was about more than that. There was something about her golden aura that touched him. He knew it—and he was almost certain she did.

Danger. Fire. And Lydia Stanford. Like the Holy Trinity they belonged together.

'Thank you.'

'Give Wendy my…' *Love.* She'd been about to say love. Hardly appropriate for a woman she didn't know. 'Best wishes.'

His hand went to his tie. 'I'll do that.'

Lydia made herself smile. She didn't know what was going on here. There were undercurrents she didn't understand. 'Perhaps she'll ring me when she feels…ready?'

'I'm sure she will.'

And then he left. Awkwardly—and she had no idea why. Why was it she felt so uncomfortable round Nicholas Regan-Phillips? It wasn't as if she wasn't used to men with influence and money. She was.

She heard the front door click shut and gazed

about Wendy Bennington's tired kitchen. *What the heck was she doing?* And, more importantly, *why* was she doing it?

It was true, what she'd told Nicholas Regan-Phillips, she did have the time. This was her holiday.

Nicholas Regan-Phillips. What a mouthful of a name. Nick Regan. *His* Nick Regan suited him far better.

Lydia filled the old limescale encrusted kettle and set it on the gas hob. It was just so out of character for her to have agreed to kick her heels in such a place.

Why would she do that? This wasn't her problem.

But Nick Regan was, that little voice that sat some way to the left of her shoulder whispered. He was arrogant, rude, supercilious…and sexy. Lydia searched around for a coffee mug. Bizarrely, Nick Regan was very, very sexy—and he was probably the reason she'd agreed to stay.

Now, if Izzy knew that…

CHAPTER THREE

SOME decisions just weren't good ones. Lydia glanced over at the cat basket, ridiculously pleased to see that Nimrod was safely locked inside.

There was no man, or woman, on earth who warranted the kind of self-sacrifice she'd endured today. Wendy's cottage was an unpleasant place to kick your heels for the best part of a day and Nimrod was the kind of cat who should be certified—and she had the scratches to prove it.

Lydia changed gear to negotiate a particularly tight bend. She'd gone wrong at the moment when she'd said it would be no problem to stay. She should have cited a mountainous pile of laundry and the possibility of a phone call from her former editor as reasons she *had* to be back in London.

Instead, she'd endured hours sitting on an uncomfortable sofa with a laptop perched on a melamine tray before being...well, here...and on her way to Nicholas Regan-Phillips's domestic empire. Though that part didn't bother her. She had to admit she had a rabid curiosity to see what it would be like.

There'd been any number of Internet articles about Drakes but Nicholas Regan-Phillips 'the man' had emerged as something of a mystery. It was pure nosiness, of course, but when fate landed you an opportunity like this one she was not the woman to let it go to waste. She was just dying to see what kind of place he called home, considered it reparation for an otherwise completely wasted day.

Another four miles and an unexpected sharp bend and the gates of Fenton Hall loomed impressively out of a quiet country lane. Lydia pulled the car to a gentle stop. The house itself was completely hidden from view. The gates were well over six feet high, tightly shut and were edged by equally high stone walls. It was taking a desire for privacy to rather extreme lengths.

She reached into her jacket pocket for his business card and came out empty. *Where had she put the blasted thing?* She leant over to pull her handbag off the back seat and flipped open the soft leather. His card was tucked in the small front pocket.

Lydia keyed in the number he'd written on the reverse and within seconds she was answered. 'Hello. I…er…I need…' she searched for the name on the business card '…I need…Christine Pearman. I'm delivering Nimrod, Wendy Bennington's cat. Mr Regan-Phillips said he'd phone…?'

'Oh, yes. Yes, of course.' The voice on the other end sounded distracted and agitated. 'I'll let you in. Can you tell me when you are inside?'

'Okay.' Lydia tossed the mobile on to her lap as the wide gates started to swing open. 'Okay, I'm through,' she said moments later.

'You haven't seen anyone, have you? No one's gone out?'

'No.'

'No one at all?'

Good grief! This was getting rather ridiculous. Lydia looked doubtfully at the receiver. If the voice at the other end belonged to Christine Pearman it sounded as if the other woman ought to be more careful about the films she watched. 'There's no one here but me.'

'If you follow the drive up, I'll meet you at the front.'

Lydia shrugged. *How bizarre.* The drive meandered gently until she stopped in front of a spectacular house. It was the kind that had been designed along the established order of what was considered beautiful. There were just the right number of windows either side of an impressive entrance. Wide steps curved up to a front door that would have made Izzy's artistic heart drool.

Conservative estimate: upwards of two million pounds worth of 'Arts and Crafts' real estate. She leant across to speak softly to Nimrod. 'Not a bad holiday pad. Quite a contrast from home.'

Lydia unfastened her seat belt and climbed out, catching sight of a beautifully manicured lawn stretching out to the side of the house. It was a stunning place. Which made it strange, surely, for such a wealthy man to leave a god-mother he loved with so little?

She lifted out the cat basket. Why not set her up with a little cottage in the grounds? There was bound to be one. Probably more than one.

'Lydia Stanford?'

Lydia spun round. 'Yes. I have... Nimrod.'

'Mr Regan-Phillips did telephone,' the other woman said with a nod. Her eyes looked past Lydia and seemed to scan the bushes behind her.

It was strange, preoccupied behaviour. She'd expected to be asked in for a cup of tea or some-thing—a chance to see inside the inner sanctum of Nicholas Regan-Phillips's impressive home. A chance to glean some snippet of information she could regale Izzy with.

Instead the housekeeper seemed completely distracted. Her face was agitated and her eyes were continually darting around as though she were searching for something.

'Are you all right?' Lydia asked abruptly.

'Yes, I...' the other woman broke off '...that is...'

There was the sound of tyres on gravel and the housekeeper looked round. 'Thank heaven!'

Lydia turned round in time to see Nicholas Regan-Phillips's dark green Jaguar twist up the drive. She watched as he climbed out of the driver's seat and slammed the door shut.

Actually, she thought dispassionately, he was sexier than she'd first thought—if that was possible. He was taller, sharper. He looked as though he was used to the world working exactly as he wished it would. And there was something incredibly attractive about that.

She watched as his housekeeper surged forward, stopping him, the hapless Nimrod still imprisoned in the cat basket. Lydia caught no more than snatches of their conversation, words carried back to her on the breeze. 'We thought she was sleeping—'

Nick looked past her and his eyes locked with Lydia's. He crossed towards her, his feet scrunching on the gravel. 'I'm sorry. It seems my daughter, Rosie, has gone missing,' he explained quietly.

Instantly Lydia's mind flew through possible options. Was it possible she'd been kidnapped?

Something of that must have shown on her face because he added, 'It's something she does quite frequently. The grounds are fully enclosed; I'm sure there's nothing to worry about.'

Lydia frowned, trying to remember what she'd read in that Internet article. She was sure his daughter had been very young, but his words seemed to suggest he was the father of a teenager. 'How old is she?'

'Five.'

Five! He was remarkably unconcerned for a man who had misplaced his *very* young child. And wasn't he divorced from her mother? No doubt she wouldn't be quite so laid back if she knew he *kept* losing their daughter.

'How long has she been missing?' he asked, turning back to the housekeeper.

Christine was considerably agitated. 'No more than forty minutes. Sophie went in and checked on her before she came down for a cup of tea. We've searched the house thoroughly—'

'And down by the lake?' he cut in abruptly.

'Arthur and Tom are there now.'

His nod was decisive, as though he approved. Lydia glanced from one to the other. He clearly didn't expect anything other than that his daughter had lost herself in the grounds—which, lake aside, was probably fine.

His housekeeper obviously disagreed. Her face was pinched with worry and she clasped and unclasped her hands. 'She packed a bag this time. She's even taken her toothbrush…' Christine broke off and searched up her sleeve for a handkerchief.

Which meant, of course, that five-year-old Rosie had made a decision to run away. Which meant she was unhappy. And, she 'kept' doing it—so she was very unhappy.

Now *that* should worry a father. Lydia glanced up at him and saw very little sign of emotion. Not much more than a flash of irritation in those clever eyes—and whether the root cause was Christine or his errant daughter she couldn't be sure.

His eyes flicked across to her…and then she understood in a sudden blinding flash of comprehension. His problem was with *her*. Or, more specifically, with her overhearing his private business.

As if she'd write anything about his daughter...

Unless, of course, she discovered he was a bad parent. That would be different, she conceded silently. Then she just might...

Or might not. She wouldn't write anything that hurt a child. And it irritated her that he didn't instinctively *know* that about her.

Lydia caught herself up on her thoughts. It didn't matter what he thought of her—or her profession. What mattered was an unhappy little girl hiding out in her father's grounds. And he ought to be looking for her.

'I'm in the way. I'll leave you to it...'

She was certain she saw a glimmer of relief. He held out his hand. 'Thank you for bringing Nimrod.'

'It's no bother,' she lied, automatically stretching out her own hand.

He had a good handshake, firm and decided, and she had the oddest sense of regret that he didn't like her. For some reason it hurt that he didn't trust her. She'd had people spit venom at her, but this bothered her more because it was so unwarranted. As far as she knew, she'd never met him before yesterday, had never met anyone who knew him well. So why?

'I've… I've put the key back under the pot.' He released her hand. Lydia reached inside her jacket pocket for her car key. 'Do let me know if there's any change with Wendy…'

He nodded.

'And—' she forced a bright smile '—I hope you find your daughter quickly.'

'Thank you. Ring to the house as before and Christine will open the gates.'

She nodded and, with a swift smile at the distraught housekeeper, Lydia turned towards her car. It was disappointing not to have seen inside his house. She'd have liked to have known whether Nick Regan-Phillips's tastes leant towards minimalism or whether he was a staunch traditionalist.

She started the engine. Probably the latter. She could imagine his home would be filled with tasteful antiques sourced by others. Dining chairs designed by Rennie Macintosh perhaps? That would suit the age of his house. He probably saw them as long-term investments rather than objects of beauty. He struck her as someone who wouldn't choose anything based on an emotional response.

Which was a shame, because he had real potential. Lydia slipped the car into second gear and glanced in her rear-view mirror in time to see him turn and walk slowly up the steps. He was sexy. In that British, uptight, public school kind of way.

Why was that so attractive? She smiled. There was something about a repressed male that made her want to roughen him up. See what was bubbling beneath the surface.

And with Nick Regan-Phillips there must be something. Drakes wasn't the kind of success that happened by chance—or even because of the old boy network. It had happened because of passion. And drive. And brilliance. There was no denying that. Whatever else he was, Nicholas Regan-Phillips was a brilliantly clever man.

Out of the corner of her eye she caught sight of a flash of red. A single glimpse of it and then it vanished behind a lush camellia. Instinctively she slowed down, her eyes searching for confirmation of what she thought she'd seen.

Rosie?

Or someone searching for her? Lydia pulled the car to a gentle stop, uncertain what she should do. This was not her concern—but when had that ever stopped her?

With sudden energy she climbed out of the car and leant on the open door. 'Rosie?'

She waited, listening closely.

'Is that you?'

There was no answer. Which either meant there was no one there or that Rosie didn't want to be found. Lydia hesitated. This was not her business and she was almost certain Nick Regan-Phillips would prefer her to leave him to deal with his missing daughter. But if she asked for the gates to be opened and Rosie slipped out she'd never forgive herself.

She shut the door and moved off the gravel path. 'Rosie? Everyone is looking for you.'

Still nothing.

Slowly she walked round a large camellia, her eyes searching for another tell-tale scarlet flash among the shrubs. 'Rosie?'

In spring and early summer, when the rhododendrons were in flower, this would be the most incredible sight, exotic and beautiful—but there was no sign of a five-year-old girl anywhere. Lydia shrugged, disappointed. She must have been mistaken.

Lydia threaded her way back along the path, but as she stepped out on to the gravel drive she saw a second flash of red. This time she didn't call out, but quickened her pace. She wasn't familiar with children, particularly those as young as five, but if this one was purposely running away from home she wasn't going to want to be found.

Nipping through a narrow gap, Lydia was surprised to find…anything. She stopped abruptly, amazed to see a child standing quietly beside the grass verge. She hesitated, uncertain what to say to a five-year-old she'd never seen before and who had run away from home. 'Are you Rosie? Everyone is searching for you.'

The little girl stared back at her. Not frightened, more curious. Lydia risked moving closer. Rosie's dark curling hair was tied up in one high pony-tail and she was wearing a bright red dress and white lacy cardigan. She looked more like a doll than a real living breathing girl.

But that was clearly a deceptive impression. Rosie obviously had a will of iron and at her feet lay an overfilled lime-green backpack to prove it.

'My name is Lydia…' she began, tailing off when she caught sight of something tucked behind Rosie's right ear. It was almost imperceptible because of the hair, but…unmistakable. Rosie wore a hearing-aid. In fact, as she looked closer she could see that she wore two.

Rosie was deaf.

Lydia stood absolutely still. Her mind worked quickly. This explained why the housekeeper was so worried. Why she'd asked whether anyone had been near when the gates had opened.

If Rosie couldn't hear when she called… And no one knew where she'd gone…

It would be a nightmare and if the little girl was determined not to be found…The grounds were extensive. It would take hours to search them properly.

She looked directly at Rosie and placed two fingers to her ear in the sign for 'deaf'.

Slowly the little girl nodded, her brown eyes wide and curious. Her fingers moved against her own ear and then pointed at her chest.

It had been a long time since Lydia had signed. A very long time. She was probably going to be very rusty, but there had to be something remaining of her first language. Her mother had used it always. It was the first memory Lydia had. Speech had come through friends and playgroup, television and social workers.

Lydia smiled and sat down on the grass verge. Making sure Rosie could see her mouth, she carefully finger-spelt L-y-d-i-a—followed by her sign name. It had been picked by her father because he thought she had bright, wide eyes. It brought back so many memories. Memories of her childhood. Friday evenings, the first in every month, spent at the local deaf club, where she had seen her parents relaxed and happy as they rarely had been outside their home.

Rosie's fingers moved rapidly and Lydia struggled to follow. She was out of practice. She picked up something about a row. At least she thought it was the sign for 'row'—it might have been 'war', but that wasn't as likely.

Why couldn't she remember?

Hating the slowness with which she had to reply, Lydia tried to tell Rosie that her father was back at the house and it was time to go home. The little girl looked thoughtful and then shook her head.

Why? Lydia made the sign on the right-hand side of her chest.

Rosie signed again. The same quick movements, but this time Lydia understood perfectly. Rosie didn't want to go home unless Lydia would tell her father why she'd run away.

To Rosie it probably seemed quite simple for a complete stranger to tell Nick Regan-Phillips why his child kept trying to escape. But Rosie was only five. She couldn't possibly understand that between adults things were much more complicated.

Nick would probably consider it interfering. Lydia thought for a moment. It couldn't matter. Even if he thought she was stepping way over the line he'd be grateful she'd brought Rosie home safely.

Lydia looked Rosie straight in the eye and signed 'yes'. Then she held out her hand and, with complete trust, Rosie put her own inside it. *Could it really be that easy?*

She glanced across at her car, wondering whether it would be right to persuade a child who didn't know her to get in it. On balance, she thought not. Of course, encouraging her to walk off with a stranger wasn't a great idea either, but what was the alternative? At least they were still within the grounds of Fenton Hall and the important thing was to get her home.

It was also important to keep her promise. She'd managed to understand Rosie enough to realise how important it was. Someone had shouted at her and Rosie was sad. The two little fingers moving rapidly across her open palm had been her running into the garden. She'd packed her bag and run away.

Slowly the long-forgotten signs were coming back.

Rosie let go of her hand and tapped her arm to draw her attention. Lydia stopped and looked down as the little girl's fingers moved more rapidly than she could hope to follow. From nowhere Lydia seemed to be able to pull the sign for 'quick'. *'Too quick,'* she told Rosie and squatted down in front of her.

And the sign for 'again'. Two bounces of the first two fingers held straight. *'Again, please.'*

Rosie's face broke into a gentle smile. Watching carefully to see she was understood, she told Lydia she didn't like Sophie. That Sophie was cross. Sophie shouted. And that she wanted to find her grandma.

Lydia nodded her understanding.

Then Rosie asked her to tell her father that she wanted Sophie to go. She didn't wait to see what Lydia would reply. She picked up her lime-green backpack and tucked her hand back inside Lydia's.

Who the heck was Sophie? And what had she done to make Rosie dislike her so much? Lydia glanced down at the tiny figure beside her. She didn't look particularly cowed by whatever Sophie had done. She looked more like a determined little thing who was very used to getting her own way.

Until she knew otherwise, she was inclined to give the unknown Sophie the benefit of the doubt, but she would tell Nick what his daughter had said. Clearly Rosie felt she needed an advocate. Now that was something she was good at.

Nick held up his hand to stop the two women talking at the same time, both more than anxious to justify why his daughter's running away hadn't been anything to do with them. *God help him.* What exactly did he pay them for if it wasn't to keep Rosie safe?

'Let's deal with all of this when we know where Rosie is. Has anyone thought to look in the summerhouse?'

Christine looked affronted. 'I looked there myself. And searched the house thoroughly. I will lay my life on it she's not inside.'

Nick nodded. He was in no mood to pander to his housekeeper's wounded pride. Sophie looked belligerent beside her. As a nanny she clearly left a great deal to be desired. She might have had the most amazing references but she was lazy. If he'd known more about Rosie's needs he wouldn't have accepted Sophie into his home in the first place. She might have all the latest theories but she didn't seem to like children very much—or maybe it was just Rosie she didn't like?

Rosie certainly didn't like her. Perhaps they were simply incompatible and it was a mutual thing. As soon as he had a moment, he'd have to look into finding a more suitable replacement. Preferably someone who was specifically used to looking after a deaf child.

Ana had said it was difficult enough finding someone who was used to respecting the privacy of the family she was employed by without adding the impossible criterion of sign language. Clearly he had to try.

He sighed. 'Let's get this straight. You put Rosie to bed early—'

'For spitting,' Sophie cut in. 'I told her that the only excuse for that kind of behaviour was that she was tired.'

Nick drew a weary hand through his hair. 'And went down for a cup of tea?'

'I left her to think about what she'd done. I—'

'And neither of you heard her come back downstairs?' They looked at each other. 'Or go out through the front door?'

'I can't understand how it had been left open. I'm sure—'

Nick held up his hand again and Christine fell into silence. 'I'm sure you can't,' he said dryly, breaking off as there was a knock at the door. 'What is it?'

A second knock and he strode over and flung open the door, his voice freezing as he saw Rosie and Lydia standing in the doorway.

Lydia smiled, her hand poised to knock again. 'I caught sight of her as I was leaving and I—'

'You've found her!' Christine let out a cry of relief and ran forward to try and hug the little girl. 'I was so worried about you.'

Rosie stood stiffly, her little face stony and totally unreceptive to the embrace. But what amazed Lydia was that Christine hadn't made sure her mouth could be lip-read. In fact she hugged the little girl so closely that her words were completely lost in Rosie's hair, regardless of how much she might have caught with the help of her hearing-aids.

Lydia looked up at Nick. 'I saw a flash of red behind a camellia bush and went to investigate.'

'Thank you. Very much.'

And it sounded as if he meant it. Having braced herself to meet with his seemingly habitual reserve, she was stunned to see the hint of moisture in his dark eyes. *He really cared.* She caught herself up on the thought. *Of course* he cared. Rosie was his daughter. What had she expected?

He drew the little girl into the sitting room and knelt down in front of her. His mouth moved clearly so Rosie could lip-read. 'We were worried about you. You mustn't go outside on your own.'

But he didn't hug her. He didn't wrap his arms

about her and tell her how much he loved her. He was stiff and awkward. Lydia wanted to thump him and tell him he was handling this all wrong. That it would take considerably more life experience than a five-year-old possessed to understand what the shimmer in his eyes meant.

And what did she know? She avoided relationships. Didn't want to become a mother because she couldn't contemplate bringing children into a world like this one. What had suddenly made her such an expert on human relationships?

She saw Rosie look away and realised that he'd lost her. She was one angry little girl and Nick had missed an opportunity to build a bridge. And he didn't even know it.

What was it about rich people's children? On the surface they had every advantage, but so often their parents didn't seem to have any real kind of relationship with them. They were put into the care of nannies and other 'professionals' before they could talk and dispatched to boarding school at the first opportunity.

She walked forward and took hold of Rosie's

hand, feeling incredibly protective. For Rosie it was even worse than for most children of wealthy parents. Her mother had told her enough of her own childhood experiences for Lydia to be acutely aware of how difficult it could be to be born deaf in a hearing family.

Rosie had asked her to speak for her—and she would. She would make sure Nick Regan-Phillips listened. More than that; as far as it was in her power she would make sure things changed.

'Rosie asked me to tell you she's been very unhappy.'

Nick looked up at her words, stunned by them. Around them there seemed to be a pool of silence.

Lydia hesitated and glanced down at Rosie. She only hoped she'd judged this right. Had judged Nick right. If Sophie was the sulky-looking twenty-something in the corner she might be about to make Rosie's life much worse.

'I gather there was some kind of argument—'

'Yes, there was.' All eyes turned to the woman she'd assumed was Sophie as she forcefully interrupted. 'I will not have defiance and—'

'Sophie—' Nick glanced over his shoulder, his voice brooking no disagreement '—the important thing is that Rosie is safe. I think we can leave everything else to the morning.'

She looked as if she might have protested, but thought better of it. 'As you wish.' Her chin became just that little bit squarer. 'It's late. I'll put her to bed.'

Sophie held out her hand, but Nick forestalled her with a decided, 'No.' His hand reached out and stroked the top of his daughter's head. It was the first real sign of affection Lydia had seen between the two—and it reminded her of how he'd been with Wendy.

He'd been gentle. Kind.

Rosie curved towards her father and Lydia knew she hadn't misjudged him. There was a good man inside that city suit…and if he just let himself go…

'I'll put Rosie to bed myself.'

Lydia heard Sophie's sharp intake of breath and judged his announcement to be unprecedented, but she waited confidently for Sophie to be sent from the room.

She had little doubt he'd do that. She'd seen the way he cared and, whatever was really going on here, she didn't believe he'd want his daughter to be shouted at and bullied by a twenty-year-old something who thought she was God's gift to childcare.

Christine Pearman might be a nice woman who could be educated to care, but Sophie…no, Sophie was not that kind of woman.

Sophie was the kind of woman who knew best—always. She'd read the book and knew all the answers. It might be the kind of snap judgement Izzy deplored, but Lydia was quite happy to keep hold of Rosie's hand in hers and wait for Nick to justify her faith in him.

She wasn't disappointed. He stood up and looked directly at Sophie as he said, 'I'm sure you've found the whole experience very stressful, so I'll take care of Rosie now. Thank you.' Then he looked across at his housekeeper. 'That will be all for now, Christine.'

'D-dinner?'

'Will need to wait until Rosie is asleep.'

Both women left the room, cowed—and he'd

not raised his voice. His words had been spoken with a quiet authority, expecting people to comply with his wishes. Lydia, used as she was to a newsroom environment and the way the air frequently turned blue, found it impressive stuff.

It was strange he didn't inspire her with that kind of awe. All she saw was a man, albeit a sexy one, who needed a great deal of help with his daughter. Or perhaps it would be more accurate to phrase it as the daughter who needed help with her father?

She saw him glance down at their still-joined hands and felt a momentary pang of pity for him. He was out of his depth and floundering.

And he looked unbearably weary. He'd had a hell of a couple of days and what she was about to say wasn't going to make his life any better—at least, not in the short-term.

'Rosie has asked me to tell you she doesn't like Sophie.'

Her words acted like a slap. She saw the effect of them on Nick as though she'd taken a whip to him.

'She told you?' His voice sounded hollow.

'Yes.'

'You sign?'

Her eyes flew to his. 'You don't?'

His eyes didn't leave her face and she saw his effort to swallow.

He didn't sign. How could the father of a deaf five-year-old not have learnt something of the method she used to communicate? It was unbelievable. Criminal.

'Well, you should. How do you expect her to talk to you?'

CHAPTER FOUR

NICK felt as if he'd been flayed on the raw. It spoke to the guilt within him. He didn't sign—and he knew he should be able to. Rosie was five years old. Since he'd been told his daughter was profoundly deaf he'd had over four years to learn.

There were reasons, of course, why he hadn't done. Good reasons. Or at least they'd seemed good until Rosie had suddenly come to live with him. And somehow, looking at Lydia's incredible amber-flecked eyes, he knew she wouldn't think his excuses good enough.

Which they weren't. He'd let his daughter down. When she'd needed him to comfort her he'd not even been able to ask what she liked to eat for breakfast. He'd been forced to pull cereal packets out of the cupboard and wait for her to either nod or shake her head. It was a form of communication, but it was limited.

Rosie had been given no alternative but to tell a complete stranger that she didn't like her nanny. What made it even worse was that he'd known that. Deep down. Or even not so deep. It had been obvious. He'd simply chosen to ignore it because it made his life simpler.

He'd argued that it gave Rosie some stability to have the same nanny she'd had when she'd lived with her mother. And Sophie was very highly qualified, with good references…

All excuses—and he knew it. Faced with his daughter's guileless brown eyes looking up at him, how could he not? And Lydia…

Her eyes told him exactly what she was thinking of him. She was looking at him with incredulity. She tossed back that incredible mane of hair, which framed a face that was more intelligent than conventionally beautiful, and her words stung him again. 'Rosie signs wonderfully. It's clearly her first language.'

'She's also able to lip-read very well,' he said defensively.

'That's not the point, though, is it? That's her understanding you, not *you* understanding her. You have a responsibility to Rosie and—'

'I'm completely aware of my responsibilities.' His voice sliced across hers, much harder than he'd intended. He resisted the impulse to apologise.

For one moment there was complete silence, during which Lydia's eyes didn't so much as flicker away from his. 'You're right,' she said at last. 'It's absolutely not my business to tell you how to raise your child, but—'

'No, it isn't.'

'But,' she continued as though he hadn't spoken, 'I made a promise to Rosie. I told her I would tell you how she feels and I fully intend to keep my promise.'

Then Lydia broke eye-contact, calmly kneeling in front of Rosie. She gently tapped his daughter on the arm and Rosie looked at her confidently, her brown eyes wide and trusting.

And it hurt.

Nick swallowed painfully. It hurt so much to

see his daughter looking to someone else to tell him what she felt. Trusting them to do it.

He felt the whip of guilt. He should have made more time. He shouldn't have left her with a nanny like Sophie. He should have fought for her when Ana had left him. *Damn it!* He should have learnt to sign and made sure he'd forged a real connection with Rosie. The regrets pounded in his head like wave after wave on a cliff face.

He scarcely knew his child. *God forgive him.* And now he needed someone to help him communicate with his own daughter.

And for that someone to be Lydia Stanford...

It hurt. So much. It was difficult to have to be grateful to a woman like Lydia. He wasn't even quite sure what kind of woman she was. How did you meld together what he'd seen of her with what he knew about her?

It was incontrovertible fact that Lydia had used every skill she possessed to ensure Steven Daly and his associates were put behind bars. Her sister's miscarriage and suicide attempt had been made public knowledge during a long and complicated court case. All manner of private details about Isabel Stanford's life had been open to public scrutiny and cross-examination—for weeks on end.

It was easy to imagine how deeply humiliating it must have been for a shy twenty-three-year-old to have her life dissected and discussed over other people's breakfast.

Day after day there'd been photographs of the sisters. Lydia had looked strong, confident and utterly determined—her sister...had looked broken.

True enough, Steven Daly was a Machiavellian character who deserved to be in prison, but...how could Lydia sleep at night knowing what she'd exposed her vulnerable sister to?

One particular image, taken outside the courtroom on the final day, stayed with him. In that photograph Lydia's sister had been completely surrounded by reporters, dwarfed by them. She'd stood with one solitary tear resting halfway down her cheek. A moment frozen in time. She'd looked emotionally battered, alone and utterly heartbroken.

Lydia might argue she'd done it all for her

sister, but he knew that wasn't true. There was no way the young, emotionally traumatised Isabel had been thinking of vengeance. She'd merely been concentrating on finding the will to stay alive.

When Wendy had told him she'd insisted Lydia Stanford was her biographer or she wouldn't co-operate, he'd been horrified. Everything he'd discovered about Lydia since then had only confirmed how single-minded she was. A woman totally focused on achieving her goals whatever the cost.

But when he'd met her...

Lydia hadn't been quite the woman he'd been expecting. She exuded a warmth he hadn't anticipated. A kindness.

If he'd simply met her...at a party perhaps? If he hadn't seen her give that interview after the jury had passed a unanimous 'guilty' verdict...

Then it would have been a very different story.

He knew he'd have been mesmerised by those incredible eyes and bewitched by the rich colours in her hair. He would have asked for her telephone number and he wouldn't have waited more than twenty-four hours before inviting her to dinner.

But beneath the attractive veneer Lydia Stanford was still a woman who passionately craved success in her chosen career—and he knew exactly what that kind of ambition was like to live with. He knew how cruel it could be—and how painful.

He watched as Lydia asked his daughter what she wanted to say. Her hands moved gracefully. She had beautiful hands with long tapering fingers and nails that were perfectly manicured. She also had a vivid scratch across the back of her right hand—no doubt a parting gift from Nimrod.

And then he had to watch as Rosie told Lydia what she *did* want to say. *Dear God.* His heart ached as he watched her tiny hands move in rapid jerky movements. Her face was full of expression as finally *his* daughter got the chance to tell him what she'd held locked inside her for all the weeks she'd lived in his home.

Rosie's little face began to crumple and he found that his feet moved and his arms locked tightly around her, his hand stroking the top of his daughter's head. Lightly kissing her curls, he rested his chin on the top of her head and looked across at Lydia. 'What did she say?'

Lydia's voice was husky as though she'd been affected by what she'd been told. Her beautiful eyes, still with the same flecks of fire in them, looked softer than he'd seen them before. 'It's complicated.'

'I imagine it is.' And suddenly it didn't matter whether Lydia Stanford was here only because she wanted a story. What really mattered, more than life itself, was Rosie.

And if Lydia was the means by which he could establish a relationship with his daughter, then he was going to welcome it—whatever the personal cost.

Rosie turned within his arms and he held her tightly, every muscle in his body striving to convey how much he loved her. As her sobs quietened, he held her away from his body and stared into her eyes, willing her to understand him.

Her eyes were so like his own. 'I'm sorry,' he

said carefully. 'Rosie...I...' And then he looked across at Lydia. 'What did she say? Why is she so unhappy? Tell me,' he prompted when she seemed to hesitate.

Lydia stood up slowly and went to sit on a nearby sofa. She usually found words easy to find. From the school notebooks she'd filled with stories of sword-wielding heroines, to her career as a journalist, she'd always found it easy to say what she meant. Communication was what she did best.

But not this time. What she had to tell Nick Regan-Phillips was going to hurt him—and she didn't want that. In the space of fifteen minutes she'd gone from thinking him a poor parent to thinking him a flawed one.

She didn't understand why a parent of a deaf child who signed would refuse to learn it, but she had no doubt that he loved his daughter. Seeing him hold Rosie was probably going to be one of those images that would stay with her all her life. Even having seen Nick with his godmother she hadn't believed him capable of such honest emotion.

Lydia cleared her voice carefully. She had to tell him the truth—exactly as Rosie had told her. 'She... She understands why she was sent here. Or thinks she does.'

Pushing back her long hair from her face, Lydia tried again. 'Rosie says she was sent here because her mother doesn't like her because she's deaf and she thinks you're too busy to have her live with you.'

A flicker of acute pain passed across Nick's face and Lydia didn't dare stop in case she lost her nerve. She'd promised Rosie. She *would* keep her promise.

'She says Sophie shouts at her because she can't hear and gets cross when she doesn't understand. She wants to go back to her grandma's house and live with her.' Lydia looked away, hating the raw look of pain on his face. 'I'm sorry. Really.'

Nick shook his head as though to absolve her from any part in his agony and then he kissed Rosie's head. His hand lightly stroked the top of her head and down the side of her cheek. 'I'm sorry.'

Then he looked at Lydia. 'How do I sign "sorry"?'

Lydia swallowed down the lump in her throat. 'You use your little finger for things that are bad.' She extended her own small finger and with the rest of her hand in a ball made small circles against her chest. ' "Sorry". It's like this.'

He moved his own hand. It wasn't perfect—but Rosie understood. She reached out and stopped him moving his hand and then tucked in for a cuddle.

It was a beginning. Perhaps more than a beginning? Perhaps it was a breakthrough?

'She understood me.' His deep voice was incredulous.

Lydia smiled, her eyes shimmering with emotion.

'Will you tell her I won't leave her with Sophie again? I can't do much about her mother or grandmother, but I will stay with her myself.'

'Don't promise her what you can't give—'

'I won't leave her with anyone she doesn't want to be with.'

If almost anyone else had made that statement

Lydia wouldn't have believed them, but Nick said it in a way that made her believe he would do exactly what he said he would. Goodness only knew what upheavals it would cause in his professional life.

Nevertheless it was the right decision. Unquestionably. Rosie needed him. It was what being a parent was all about. Selfless love.

As an onlooker Lydia could see it clearly. It was why she never wanted children of her own. She wasn't capable of selfless love. She never wanted to be in a position where she'd have to choose between what she wanted to do and what other people needed her to do.

Who was it who said it was a wise man who knew his limitations? Well, that applied equally well to women. She knew she could never subjugate her desires to the needs of another. She was too selfish. She hadn't been able to do it at eighteen and there was no reason to suppose she could ever do it in the future.

Lydia tapped Rosie on the shoulder. The little girl turned round. She could see from her hopeful expression that she trusted her father.

Carefully she signed out what Nick had said. Rosie glanced at him and Nick nodded in confirmation.

Then Rosie smiled, her tiny heart-shaped face lit up with a beauty that defied the tear-stains. Seeing it, Lydia felt her own heart contract. If that expression didn't reward Nick for doing the right thing, then nothing would.

For the second time in as many days Lydia felt an outsider. She was a bystander to an emotional connection she wasn't part of. An onlooker. Not really needed.

It wasn't as if she really knew Nick Regan-Phillips and his daughter. She was here purely because of a series of circumstances and the sooner she left the better. Witnessing this kind of connection made her aware of an ache within herself. The emptiness and a longing for something more in her life. Something career success didn't give her.

Lydia stood up and, the minute she did so, Rosie turned. She stretched out her hand. Lydia took it in her own, but with her one free hand signed that she must go home.

The little girl vehemently shook her head.

Nick stood up a little shakily. 'I don't think she's ready to lose you.'

'I—'

'Have you eaten?'

It was such an abrupt change of subject that Lydia frowned in an effort to make sense of it.

'Eaten. I asked if you'd eaten yet?' he repeated slowly. 'After everything you've done for me today the least I can do is offer you dinner.'

'No, I haven't.' In fact, since Izzy's spectacular and totally sinful fried breakfast, she'd not eaten anything but the half packet of chocolate biscuits she'd tucked in the glove compartment of her car.

'Then stay for dinner.'

'But Christine Pearman won't be expecting another mouth to feed…'

'Christine is paid to expect the unexpected,' he said with all the old arrogance she disliked. How could he make a statement like that? Didn't he know that meals couldn't conjure themselves out of thin air? That they required planning and preparation before they appeared on the table?

But then Lydia thought of her empty flat. Her two close friends exploring Vienna without her. What was there to rush back to London for?

It was tempting to stay. Rosie tugged on her hand and Lydia felt herself weaken. 'Are you sure?'

'Yes.'

She looked up into Nick's dark brown eyes and thought what a staggeringly complicated man he was. He was also fascinating. It was at that moment that she knew she'd stay.

'I'll need to stay with Rosie until she's asleep, but then we could…talk.'

Her eyes moved to his mouth. *Talk.* Hmm, yes. They *could* talk. Did he know he had the sexiest mouth? Or that his lips would be described as firm and sensual in a romance novel? And then there was that slight indentation in the centre of his chin. She'd read somewhere that it was indicative of a sensual personality.

Who knew whether that was true, but looking at Nick Regan-Phillips you kind of suspected it might be. Lydia pulled her eyes away from his face, horrified at where her thoughts had taken her.

'You've obviously got some experience of being in contact with deaf people. I'd like to hear your suggestions for what would help Rosie.'

'Of course.' Put like that, how could she refuse?

'I'll ask Christine to bring you a drink through to the sunroom. Or even on the terrace, since it's been a lovely day.'

Lydia looked down at Rosie, who was staring up at her with wide eyes. *She must have been so lonely.* As the thought popped into her mind she realised that anything she could do to help Rosie she would do. It had been a long time since anyone had looked at her with such blatant adoration. Even if it was only the hero-worship of a five-year-old—it felt really good.

'Actually,' Lydia said, looking round for where she'd dropped her handbag, 'I've left my car halfway down your drive. I think I'll walk down and fetch it.'

'Okay. I'll ask Christine to watch for you and I'll meet you on the terrace in…' He glanced down at his watch.

'When Rosie is asleep.'

Nick's smile was swift. 'When Rosie is asleep,' he agreed.

She watched the two of them leave the room. They looked like one of those arty photographs of a dad walking along with his little girl. Certainly Rosie was pretty enough to be a child model. She had one of those symmetrical faces and huge speaking eyes.

Her mother must be a very beautiful woman. Lydia glanced around the room. There were no photographs—although that was to be expected. They were divorced, after all. It would be very unusual if there had been any.

But she was curious to know who the enigmatic Nick would have married. If she'd anticipated any part of the events of today she'd have spent longer on the Internet and discovered who it had been.

Lydia spotted her handbag tucked next to a red cushion and went to pick it up, just as Rosie burst back into the room. The question on her lips died the minute she saw the little girl's face. Lydia crouched down and received a resounding kiss on the cheek. Slightly moist, but completely perfect.

For the first time in her life Lydia thought it might be nice to have a child of her own one day. Someone who would love her unconditionally—and then she brought herself up short. She totally disapproved of people who had children for reasons like that. If she wanted unconditional love it would be better to get a dog. And she hadn't even got space in her life for one of those.

Standing up, Lydia signed 'goodnight'. That brought back memories too. Her mother had always signed the same thing every night. *'Goodnight. Sleep tight. Don't let the bedbugs bite.'* It was almost painful to remember. It was as though she'd blocked so many of those happy memories because of the ache they brought with them.

Rosie smiled shyly and then bounced from the room. The child's whole body language had altered in the short time she'd known her. The truly astounding thing was how little it had actually taken to have wrought such a change.

Nick had to be able to see that for himself. His

daughter had simply needed to be listened to. Nothing earth-shattering about that. Everybody needed to be listened to. Lydia picked up her handbag. And then she wondered a little more about the former Mrs Regan-Phillips. What kind of woman was she? Would she object to the summary removal of the nanny she'd presumably chosen?

It wasn't her problem. She had to remember that. It was time she started to let other people fight their own battles. Izzy had said that yesterday.

Izzy.

Why hadn't she thought of that before? She needed to telephone her sister. Izzy was a teacher for special needs children. She might even know of someone who would be a perfect nanny for Rosie. Lydia started to fumble in her handbag for the cellphone as Christine came back into the room.

'Do you want me to show you out? Mr Regan-Phillips says you are bringing your car back up to the house.'

Lydia's hand, still in her handbag, closed around her mobile. 'Yes. Yes, I am.'

The older woman seemed to be a picture of cool control. If she hadn't seen her so flustered she wouldn't have believed it possible for this woman ever to be ruffled. 'I'll watch for your car and will take you through to the terrace as soon as you return.'

'Thank you.'

Together they walked along the hallway with its beautifully nourished oak floor. Lydia couldn't help but think how many hours it must take to keep it looking like this. Christine opened the heavy front door and held it wide.

Lydia paused on the top step as a thought occurred to her. She turned back. 'I hope my staying isn't too inconvenient for you.'

The housekeeper's mouth almost stretched to a smile but stopped short. 'It's not a problem.'

'Good.' Lydia skipped down the steps and started down the path towards her car. Glancing quickly over her shoulder to make sure Christine Pearman had returned inside, she pulled her mobile from her handbag and dialled her sister's number.

'Izzy?'

Her sister's voice sounded happy. 'Where are you? I've been trying to reach you for the last hour—'

'I know—' Lydia cut her off '—I've had my mobile turned off.'

'Why?'

'That's not important. Just listen to what's happened to me.'

Nick sat on the edge of Rosie's bed, watching her eyes close. Every so often she would force them open to check he was still there. Each time he smiled and gently closed her eyelids with his hand.

She was so lovely. *His* little girl. He'd hoped she'd been too young to fully appreciate what had gone on with her mother. It seemed she knew too much of some things and not enough of others.

Ana wasn't a bad person, just selfish. She wouldn't have actively wanted her daughter to be hurt. Perhaps that was why she'd not told Rosie that her grandma had died. She probably thought Rosie was too young to understand what was going on around her. How wrong Ana had been.

Rosie might not have picked up on everything, but she was in no doubt that her father was too busy for her and her mother didn't like her being deaf. Nick shook his head as though to rid himself of the thought and watched as his daughter fell into sleep. What kind of long-term damage did that do to a child?

He didn't know. *Damn it!* Nick reached out and stroked back Rosie's soft curls. It didn't matter any more. Whatever happened now, things were going to change.

Nick stood up quietly and turned off the main light, leaving the soft night-light on. He hadn't thought before how terrifying it must be for a deaf person to be left entirely in the dark. There was so much he hadn't considered. Rosie's world was completely different from his. Her experiences, now and as an adult, would be different.

He ran a hand across his neck tiredly. It was the first time in his life when he wasn't sure he had what it took. Could he learn to be a good father? He smiled. Wendy would be amazed if she ever heard him say that. Knowing her, she'd probably think it was the beginning of wisdom.

'Is the little girl asleep?' Christine Pearman asked, coming up the stairs, towels in her hand.

'Rosie is, yes.' It was time they stopped thinking of her as a 'little girl' and started thinking of her as a fully formed human being, with needs and deep-seated worries of her own.

'Would you like me to listen out in case she wakes? Sophie has gone out to a movie. I think she assumed you'd given her the evening off…'

Nick stopped with his hand on the banister rail. 'That would be excellent. Thank you. Has Ms Stanford returned to the house yet?'

'No.' The housekeeper hesitated. 'I think she had a phone call to make. Sir, do you think this is a good idea? Ms Stanford is a journalist and you've always resisted—'

'Lydia Stanford is Wendy's choice of biographer. And since Wendy is coming to stay, I think you and I ought to get used to the idea of having Ms Stanford around.'

'Yes, sir.'

'And, considering everything she's done for me today, I think the least I can do is offer her a meal.'

Christine shifted the towels in her arms. 'Of course, sir.'

She walked down the landing, leaving Nick alone to wonder why Lydia Stanford had needed to make a call. Why she'd waited until she was out of the house.

Nick turned back to his bedroom and went through to his dressing room. He needed to get out of this suit. He tore off his rich burgundy silk tie and then hung it neatly in between red and purple ones on his colour-coded tie rack.

Was this a good idea? His fingers paused on the top button of his shirt.

Almost certainly this was not a good idea. Lydia Stanford was an ambitious woman. But, he argued, this was a thank you meal. A chance to learn more about the deaf world his daughter would inhabit. It was not a chance to get to know a woman who made him want to slowly undress her and throw her blasted Anastasia Wilson jacket out of a top floor window.

He swore softly. As long as he remembered that nothing was sacred to Lydia Stanford, he'd be all right.

CHAPTER FIVE

LYDIA stood on the terrace, but given the choice she would have preferred to wait for Nick inside. It had been a pleasantly warm day rather than hot and now it was beginning to cool down still further.

The view, though, was spectacular. Everything about this house was spectacular. The lawn reached out in a gentle swathe to a wooded area below and continued on to what looked like a walled garden. In between there were huge specimen trees that had been allowed to grow to full maturity. Plenty of places for Rosie to hide from a nanny she disliked.

'She's asleep.'

Lydia turned at the sound of Nick's voice. Her first thought was that he'd changed out of his suit and into more casual clothes. Her second was that it was totally unfair.

He wore black jeans which hugged thighs that belonged on a professional sportsman, a white T-shirt and a thick charcoal-coloured over-shirt. The effect was electric. She, by contrast, was still in the clothes she'd left London i n yesterday.

'Has Christine given you a drink?'

Lydia shook her head. 'I didn't want one. I have to drive back to London tonight.'

'It's getting cold out here. Shall we go back inside?'

Gratefully she moved towards the house. 'The end of summer already. It's sad, isn't it?'

'Doesn't last long,' he agreed.

Their conversation seemed formal and awkward, as though neither of them knew quite what they were allowed to talk about. They were not friends, Lydia reminded herself. Their relationship could only be described, at best, as uneasy.

'It's a fabulous garden,' she observed, stepping through fully open glass doors that folded back to completely merge inside and outside spaces.

'It's my passion and why I bought this house. There's a little over six acres here and yet I can be in the centre of London within an hour.'

'It's very convenient,' she agreed as he led her through the reception room and across the hallway to a formal dining room.

It was exquisitely decorated although in slightly too heavy a style for her taste. The walls were papered in what she recognised to be an original William Morris design. The dining table was a rich oak and surrounded by the Rennie Macintosh chairs she'd imagined he'd own.

A traditional man in a traditional home. She loved it when people met her expectations. There was something so comforting about it.

'So,' she said brightly, 'how long have you lived here? And have you done much to the garden?'

'A little over two years. And—' he smiled '—not as much as I would like.'

'Spoken like a true gardener.' Lydia slipped off her jacket and laid it across the back of one of the chairs.

'Would you like to hang that up?' Nick asked,

pulling out one of the chairs so that she could sit down. An old-fashioned gesture which suited the image she was building of him.

'I'm sure it'll be fine there. I might as well hang on to it in case I want to go out later and inspect what you've done.'

His mouth quirked into a smile. Her stomach did a little flip in recognition. It was a sexy smile and its power was increased by the fact that it came almost without any warning. She could imagine it could easily become something of an obsession to see how often she could make them happen.

Nick took the seat at the head of the table, immediately to the left of her. It was already laid for two, with fresh rolls and small curls of cold butter in tiny round dishes. 'I believe we're to have Celeriac Soup followed by Haddock Fillets with Coriander and Lemon Pesto.'

'Don't you know? I imagined you'd give your orders in the morning and the staff would…'

'It's too big a house to manage alone,' he replied neutrally. She had to admire him for refusing to rise to her bait.

'How disappointing! I was hoping for something much more "lord of the manor".'

Nick laughed. His face relaxed and Lydia felt her stomach clench. Sexy. The man was just sexy. Maybe breaking into Wendy Bennington's house had been a very good idea.

'It's difficult to get abject obedience past the unions these days.'

Christine walked in with a large tray, setting it down on an oak sideboard.

'Ms Stanford—' Nick began.

'Lydia, please.'

'And I'm Nick.'

It seemed a little late in the day to be deciding on using first name terms, but then she realised it was because she'd been thinking of him as Nick for a while. Yet neither of them had used the other's name in conversation. *How strange.*

'Lydia,' he continued smoothly, 'was wondering how much say I have over what I eat.'

Christine set the bowls in front of them. 'It would be lovely if he took an interest. He only cares about his garden. I think I could serve the same meal every night and he wouldn't notice.'

Nick raised an eyebrow as his housekeeper left. 'Well, there you have it.'

'I think you've offended her. You must make a mental note to show more appreciation,' Lydia teased. She picked up her soup spoon. 'What do you plan to do here? With the garden?'

'Actually I'm still undecided.' Nick picked up the bottle of wine which sat in an elegantly twisting silver coaster. 'Wine?'

'A very little.'

'You're driving,' he said with a smile. 'I remember.'

He made even that seem sexy. This was beginning to feel like a date. It was so strange. Yesterday she'd have said he wouldn't have given her the time of day. *Well, he hadn't.*

He'd been rude, arrogant and supercilious. She was almost beginning to forget that.

'Currently I'm working on creating a traditional kitchen garden inspired by the one at Audley End. In Essex.'

Lydia nodded. 'I know it.'

'I've put in some espalier trees and I'm currently building some raised beds.'

'You are?' she said, surprised. 'You're doing the work yourself?'

He smiled again. 'No enjoyment if you don't. That's what I'd intended doing yesterday, only I spent most of it at the hospital with Wendy.'

Lydia looked at him. That explained the scruffy clothes when she'd first met him. She would never have suspected he'd be a gardener. Somehow that didn't quite fit with a man who'd made millions from electrical components.

But then nothing about him really fitted with her idea of a man who'd devoted his life to electrical components. Nick had the kind of voice you'd listen to even if he was reading you the telephone directory and a body...that a nicely brought-up girl would do better not to think about.

And he was a gardener. She smiled. As far as her father had been concerned, that automatically put someone on the side of good, whatever indications there might be to the contrary.

'Actually, I agree.' Her dad had never been able to understand why anyone would spend a fortune on having a garden designed for them when the whole pleasure was in getting involved, actually getting your hands dirty.

She saw Nick's gaze move to her manicured nails and laughed. 'Not that I've done much gardening recently, I admit.'

His smile broadened and Lydia looked away quickly. *She had to stop this.* The slightly uneven tilt of his mouth and the glint in his eyes had really started to do something to her. Izzy had said he was 'her type' and, despite all her protestations to the contrary, Lydia was beginning to wonder whether that was true.

Only physically, of course. She liked successful men, but she preferred them to be entirely self-made success stories. There was a hint of the silver spoon about Nicholas Regan-Phillips which meant she could have nothing in common with him. No one in her state comprehensive had had a double-barrelled name and, if they had, they'd quickly have pretended they didn't.

Which reminded her. Nick had done just that. 'Do you mind if I ask you a question?'

She fancied his eyes narrowed slightly. 'Not if I can reserve the right not to answer.'

'Deal.' Lydia picked up her soup spoon. 'Why did you tell me your name was Nick Regan?'

'Because it is.'

'Evasive. Why did you drop the Phillips part?'

His eyes crinkled in an acknowledgement of a hit. 'Your reputation went before you. I didn't want you to do what you did.'

'What did I do?' she asked, bemused.

'Find out who I was. Search me out on the Internet.'

Lydia sipped her soup. 'You were unlucky. There wasn't another Nick Regan so you were the closest match I could find. There was nothing much there, though. I'd have to go to much greater trouble to unearth any really interesting information. So far I've not found a skeleton in the closet.'

There was a small beat of silence and Lydia wondered whether she'd offended him. As ever it was difficult to tell. His face gave so little away as to what he was thinking. She'd meant the 'skeleton in the closet' bit to be a harmless quip, but perhaps it hadn't been the most sensitive thing to say. Particularly since one of the few things she did know about him was that he valued his privacy.

She took another sip of soup and was relieved when he said mildly, 'My turn to ask a question.'

'Fair enough.'

'What stopped you gardening?'

Lydia put down her spoon and picked up her wineglass. It was a simple enough question, but there were so many ways of answering it. The completely honest answer would be that her parents had died and the family house had been sold. She'd driven past it a year ago and her father's lovingly cultivated flower garden had all but vanished.

'Well…' her fingers moved along the stem of her wineglass '…I suppose university. Then work.'

'You don't have a garden in London?'

'I have a balcony.' Lydia smiled. 'And I'm the proud owner of two hanging baskets. You can't judge me by that, though. I assure you I do know my *Choisya ternata* from my *Campanula lactiflora*.'

'I'm impressed.'

He seemed to watch her from behind his wine-glass. It was actually quite unnerving to be so unsure of what someone was thinking of you. And he was thinking something. Lydia returned to her soup and let the mild celery flavour of the celeriac swirl about her mouth for a moment, then looked up. 'I had a gardening childhood.'

Nick said nothing. It had the effect of making her want to fill the silence. Lydia pulled off a piece of the bread roll and carefully smeared on some butter. 'My father was a gardener. Professionally, I mean. He loved it. Some of my earliest memories are of helping him prick out seedlings.'

Lydia looked back fondly through the years. She'd loved being with him. Had loved the magic way he'd taught her to watch for the seasons. The Saturdays spent at his allotment and the joy of bringing home freshly dug new potatoes. One day, she promised herself, one day she'd move out of London, have a garden again.

'Loved? As in past tense?'

'He…died when I was eighteen.'

'I'm sorry.'

Lydia shrugged, trying to appear nonchalant. 'It was a long time ago.' But it still hurt. The suddenness of it. 'My parents were hit by a lorry while crossing the road. My father died instantly, my mother a week later in hospital from internal injuries.'

Why was she saying this? She never told people this. Never tried to describe what it had felt like to be eighteen and have the police tell you your parents had been involved in a fatal accident. Or how responsible she'd felt taking her twelve-year-old sister to the hospital, the days of waiting for their mother to die.

She never spoke of how much she'd resented missing her school leavers' ball and how ashamed she was of that feeling. Or of her decision to go to university and break up what was left of her family unit. No amount of success, it seemed, could ever assuage the guilt of that.

Nick tore a mouthful off his own roll and said nothing. Why didn't he say something? He *should* say something, if only to be polite.

'They were deaf,' she stated baldly, filling the void. Wanting to provoke some kind of real reaction. 'The road markings had changed and they were looking the wrong way...and, of course, they didn't hear the lorry approaching.'

'And you're still angry?'

His question brought her up short. *Angry? Was she?* 'I don't blame the lorry driver...I just think it was a meaningless waste.' She sat back in her chair. 'My mum wasn't even forty when she died.'

'That's young.'

'Too young.'

Nick watched the colour of her eyes change, almost as if they really did have fire in their depths. There was anger there, he was sure of it. His own mother had died at twenty-three. But from illness. Did that make it better or worse? He wasn't sure.

He didn't have a single memory of his mother. Not one. It would have been nice to have remembered something. Nice, too, to have felt he'd known his father.

Nick watched as Lydia brushed her hair off her

neck. She often did that, it seemed, but it was completely unconscious—and that made it so much harder to resist. It drew his eyes to the soft skin of her neck before her hair fell back in a soft cascade of rich honey-coloured silk.

He looked away and was grateful when Christine returned to take away the empty soup bowls. 'Has Rosie woken at all?'

The housekeeper's face almost stretched into a smile. 'There's not been a peep out of the little mite. It looks like she might have settled for the night.'

'Does she normally wake up?' Lydia asked, the haunted look in her eyes vanishing like morning mist.

It was Nick's turn to shrug. It was the kind of question he'd no intention of answering because of where it might lead. 'She's not used to the house.'

'Doesn't she stay with you often?'

Nick looked up and met her eyes. He could read the criticism in hers easily enough, but he wasn't prepared to bare his soul to this woman. This was touching on very personal ground and he'd no intention of being newspaper fodder again.

He moved to top up her wineglass, but Lydia forestalled him. 'No more, or I'll be over the limit.'

Nick filled up his own glass as Christine put plates of fish in front of them and a serving dish of lightly cooked vegetables in the centre. 'Thank you.'

'Yes, thank you. This looks completely wonderful, Christine.'

Lydia reached out and spooned a selection of vegetables, the long scratch on her hand very noticeable.

'That looks nasty,' Nick observed.

She pulled her hand back and looked at her injury. 'Wendy was quite right when she told you Nimrod didn't like going in his cat basket. He fought like a mighty hunter.' Nick watched her run her finger along the length of the scratch and then she looked up and smiled. 'I haven't seen him since I delivered him. I hope you haven't lost him.'

He forced an answering smile. 'He'll be around.'

She was completely beguiling. The way she moved, spoke, laughed… Hell, her laugh ripped through him so he didn't know whether it was morning or evening.

What was it about him that made him fall for completely the wrong woman—always? He'd built a multi-million-pound business on recognising talent and building a team. His contemporaries rated his judgement, but when it came to women…

'How is Wendy?' she asked suddenly, giving him something concrete to focus on.

He watched the way she pulled her hand through her shining hair and saw it splay out on the black cotton of her blouse. He had read something about what it meant when a woman touched her hair. The trouble was he couldn't remember whether it meant she was or wasn't attracted to the person she was talking to.

Of course, it could just mean she didn't like her hair across her face. When he'd first seen her she'd had it tied up in that sexy waterfall-type thing. On balance, he thought he preferred it loose.

'I don't suppose you've had a chance to visit her in hospital today,' Lydia continued. 'Do you know when she'll be out?'

'Actually, I'd been to visit her before I came home tonight.' Nick picked up his wineglass and sipped, trying to concentrate on what she was saying rather than the way her mouth moved. *He had to stop this.* Concentrate on the facts. Focus on something entirely matter-of-fact.

'So, how was she?'

'She's made a complete recovery from the TIA. Scans show nothing to be concerned about.'

'That's good.'

Nick let himself smile. 'But she's to consider it a warning. They want her to cut down on her unhealthy fats and…give up smoking.'

He loved the way her smile broadened, the sexy glint that coloured her brown eyes. 'Does Wendy have a bad habit?'

'Again—' he paused to cut into his fish '—it depends on who you're speaking to. Wendy says not. She says she smokes for relaxation and it's not an addiction. Her doctor, on the other hand, considers twenty cigarettes a day something to be concerned about.'

Lydia's nose wrinkled in an attractive look of concentration. 'That's quite a lot.'

'Most worrying of all, she'll be staying here while she's trying to give up.'

And then Lydia laughed her low, husky chuckle. 'I gather she's a determined woman.'

'Like steel, though in this case it could work either way. Currently, I'm not convinced she thinks it's something she needs to do.'

'And her ankle?' Lydia speared a softly glazed baby carrot with her fork before looking up at him.

'They managed to persuade Wendy that the risk of arthritis if it didn't heal properly was significant enough to warrant surgery. Someone there must have a silver tongue because she was adamant she didn't want that.'

'Is it painful?' Her eyes clouded with sudden sympathy.

'It's a fairly standard practice, though I imagine it's not comfortable for the patient.

They've made an incision on one side of her ankle and held the bone together with screws and plates.'

'Is she in plaster?'

He nodded. 'She's in a cast up to her knee.'

'How long for?'

'Approximately six weeks. But, obviously, she'll be able to go home before then. She's agreed to spend two weeks here and after that it's negotiable.'

Lydia smiled, gave another flick of her incredibly rich hair. 'This topping on the haddock is amazing. I've never thought of making a pesto with anything other than basil, but coriander works fantastically well.'

'Are you a keen cook?'

She pulled a face. 'Yes and no. I dabble, but I don't usually have much time for it. The genius in my family is Izzy. She's as passionate about cooking as you are about your garden.'

Izzy must be Isabel. Nick felt his muscles tense at the mention of her sister's name. He hadn't expected that Lydia would mention her. Certainly not with a voice that rang with affection.

Lydia looked up, blithely unaware. 'She's my sister. You know how some people can make pastry and it's just lighter than anybody else's? Well, that's Izzy. I gave up competing.'

'Are you close to your sister?'

'Very.' Lydia stretched out her hand for the jug and poured herself some water into an empty tumbler. 'We weren't always. There's six years between us, which was too big a gap when we were children, but when Izzy was…oh, I don't know…about seventeen, the age-gap ceased to matter.' She sipped her water. 'How about you? Do you have any brothers or sisters?'

'No.'

Lydia looked up over the rim of her glass. *That didn't surprise her.* If anyone had had 'only child' stamped on his forehead it had to be Nicholas Regan-Phillips. 'Did you want any?'

'It was never an option.' His hand clenched slightly on the stem of his wineglass, an outward sign that he hadn't liked her question.

When it came to Wendy or, more specifically, Wendy's *physical condition*, Nick spoke freely—but touch on anything remotely personal and he clammed up. She looked at him speculatively. There were so many things she wanted to know about him, but it didn't seem worth upsetting him. Not when she still hoped to talk to his godmother about her life.

'Well,' she said brightly, bringing her knife and fork together in the centre of her plate and sitting back, 'I'm very glad to have my sister. Particularly since she gave me a bed for the night yesterday.'

'She lives near here?'

Lydia nodded. 'Reasonably. After I'd pointed the ambulance in the direction of Wendy's cottage, I decided to drive over and see her.'

His fingers moved ceaselessly on his wine-glass. It was quite distracting. 'Doesn't she work?'

She forced her eyes to look up. 'Pardon?'

'Your sister? I asked if she worked. It's mid-week…'

Lydia suddenly clicked. 'Not during the school holidays. She's a teacher. I don't know what she'd planned for yesterday, but she took me in with good grace and we had a chance to gossip.'

Mostly about him. Lydia let her smile broaden. It was tempting to tell him that Izzy thought he bore a strong resemblance to the actor who'd played Fitzwilliam Darcy in the recent film. It would have been fun to have seen his reaction.

Mentioning Izzy, though, had reminded her why she'd been invited to stay for dinner. *Rosie.* She mustn't waste this opportunity to do something useful.

'How often does Rosie stay with you?' she asked him as Christine came in the room with an empty tray to clear the table. Lydia saw the glance that passed between the housekeeper and her employer, but couldn't fathom why.

'This is her permanent home.'

'With you?'

'Yes.'

His answer came as a complete surprise. She'd read that his daughter lived with her mother. There was some excuse for his inability to communicate with Rosie if she only made bi-weekly visits. But if this was her permanent home… there was no excuse at all.

Lydia waited while Christine brought in apple

and pear tart as dessert and placed a jug of double cream on the table. Nick reached out and touched his housekeeper's arm. 'Thank you for keeping an ear out for Rosie. I'm grateful.'

'It's my pleasure.'

'But you're off duty now. I'll check on her from now on so you can watch your Agatha Christie programme in peace.'

Christine smiled. 'I'll see you in the morning, sir.'

Lydia toyed with her spoon, waiting for the moment when Christine shut the dining room door behind her. 'Then why don't you sign?' she asked quietly.

She watched the muscle in the side of his jaw pulse, but he didn't answer. 'It isn't difficult to learn,' she offered, thinking perhaps he was nervous for some reason.

Nick glanced across at her briefly and then looked away. Clearly he was searching for the words he wanted to say. 'Her living with me is...a recent development.'

That fitted in with what she'd read, but she needed more information before she could understand what Rosie's needs were. 'Where did she live before?' It was like chipping away at granite. 'Nick?'

'With her mother.'

She willed him to say more. 'Who taught her to sign?'

Nick reached out for his wineglass, his natural sceptism returning. 'Is this relevant?'

Lydia put down her spoon and sat back in her chair. 'It is to Rosie. She's not some kind of package you can pass between you. She's deaf. She appears to sign very well and it's cruel to leave her with no one she can talk to in her own language.'

'I know.' His voice was quiet, but it demanded to be heard. 'I will organise something.'

'When?' Lydia waited, but he clearly had no intention of answering her. 'Nick, you asked me to stay. You said you wanted to talk about ways to help Rosie, so I stayed. But every question I ask you blank. Or you give me a monosyllabic answer which, to be frank, is really irritating me.'

The muscle pulsed once more in the side of his

face. It was the only indication that he'd heard her. 'Would you like some more wine?'

'No.'

Nick put the wine bottle down carefully in the centre of the coaster. 'I never talk about my personal life.'

She blinked at the unexpectedness of his reply. She knew, of course, that he hadn't this evening. He'd been the one to ask the questions and, very unusually, she'd told him some of the most painful things about her life. Things she rarely told anyone.

'Why?'

'I consider it private.'

Lydia frowned. 'If we're not going to talk about Rosie, then why am I still here?'

She watched as he poured cream liberally over his tart and then offered her the jug. Lydia shook her head. It all looked completely delicious, but she didn't feel like eating any more.

It had been a long and very uncomfortable day and the truth was she'd really had enough of it. Now she wasn't quite so hungry and the commuter traffic was off the road, she was ready to go home. A little bit of solitude, a power shower and her own bed seemed a better option than continuing with this pointless conversation.

'I'm quite happy to discuss the merits of British Sign Language over Sign Supported English and residential deaf schools versus semi-integrated deaf units. What I'm not prepared to do is talk to you about the custody arrangements Ana and I have made.'

Now that was why he was so successful in business. Clear, concise and sparing no one. Lydia felt her hands clamp tightly together in her lap. Few men had ever made her so mad. Christopher Granger, her first editor, was one exception, but this came a really close second—and she was being irritated in her own time.

'It's a pity Rosie isn't able to compartmentalise her life as easily. Whether or not you want to discuss "custody arrangements" with me doesn't change the huge impact they have on your daughter's life.'

'I understand that.'

'Do you?' Lydia asked, warming to her task.

'You've got a daughter asleep upstairs whose observation is that her mother doesn't like her and her father is too busy for her. Perhaps you ought to consider letting her live with the grandma she loves so much.'

As soon as the words left her mouth she wondered whether she'd hit a bit below the belt. She couldn't help but see the flicker of pain pass across his eyes. Sometimes she didn't think before she engaged her mouth. 'I'm sorry. I shouldn't have said that…'

Nick sat back in his chair. 'She's dead.'

Lydia's startled eyes flew to his face.

'She died this summer.'

'Rosie doesn't know?'

Nick shook his head. 'To be honest, I didn't know she didn't until today. I would have thought Ana would have told her.'

'Clearly not,' Lydia replied bluntly. 'Maybe she found it too painful. You're going to have to tell Rosie yourself.'

He met her eyes.

'Try imagining what's going through Rosie's head right now. No wonder she keeps trying to run away. She must be so confused. Did her grandma sign?'

'I imagine so.'

'You don't know?' Lydia asked, mystified why he wouldn't know the answer to a simple question like that. She was beginning to wonder what kind of 'custody arrangements' Nick and his ex-wife had for Rosie.

His face seemed completely shuttered. It seemed to her he was morbidly afraid of sharing any part of himself with anyone. Maybe he was uncomfortable talking to her and would be better with a professional carer.

'Doesn't Rosie have a social worker you could discuss this with? I know my parents worked with several very good ones who helped them enormously,' she said, thinking out loud.

Still nothing.

Or maybe his problem was specifically with her? Yesterday she'd been convinced he didn't like her at all. She'd been so concerned for Rosie she'd forgotten his earlier assumption that she might write something that would hurt his god-mother. Perhaps this was all about that?

She finally lost patience. Lydia leant over the side of her chair and picked her handbag off the floor. 'Look, I don't think there's much point to this—'

'Please, finish your meal.'

She put her linen napkin beside her untouched plate and stood up.

Nick was on his feet. 'Would you like a coffee?'

'I don't think so.' Lydia draped her jacket over her arm. 'For the record, I'm not nearly as interested in your personal life as you think I am.'

She wondered for a moment whether he was going to protest, but she ploughed on regardless. 'You're clearly fixated by the fact that I'm a journalist, but the only information I've read about you told me your name and that you invented an electrical component which, frankly, I thought made dull reading. You've got an interesting godmother and a delightful daughter. Let's leave it at that, shall we?'

Lydia turned to leave and Nick reached out to stop her, his hand resting on her arm. She looked down pointedly and he removed it. 'I'm sorry.'

'It's not important.' And then, 'Oh, I forgot.' She reached round for her handbag and opened the flap. 'I spoke to my sister about Rosie. I hope you don't mind.' Lydia pulled out a small notebook and ripped the front page out. 'I told you she's a teacher?'

Nick nodded.

'She's a specialist teacher, so I rang her. I thought she might know of some useful contacts. Anyway,' she said, handing over the piece of paper, 'I jotted down the numbers she gave me.'

'Thank you.' His voice sounded tight and constrained.

'She also said she might know of a nanny who might suit your daughter—if, of course, you and...Ana decide on replacing Sophie. Izzy's happy to speak to you if you want to ring her. Her telephone number is on the back.'

She saw him look down at the piece of paper as though he wasn't quite sure what to make of it. *Well, that was his problem now.* She'd done everything she could do to help Rosie.

Lydia tucked the notepad back inside her

handbag and flicked it shut. Turning abruptly, she walked confidently from the dining room, aware that Nick was close behind her. At the front entrance she stopped and waited while he opened the door.

'Lydia—'

She held out her hand. 'Goodbye. Please thank Mrs Pearman for cooking such a delicious supper. I appreciated it.'

Nick took her hand and held it firmly. 'Lydia, I'm sorry if I've offended you—'

'Not at all.'

'It wasn't intentional. And thank you for everything you've done today. For bringing the cat here. And for Rosie...'

'You're welcome.'

Lydia shivered in the night air and slipped her arms into her jacket. She adjusted the collar and set her handbag back on her shoulder. Halfway down the steps she turned and looked back up at him. 'You know, you could have trusted me.'

'I don't trust anyone.'

Which just about said it all. Lydia turned and walked towards her car. If it was true that he trusted no one then it was one of the saddest things she'd ever heard—and such a waste.

Was it money that had done that to him?

Or life? Perhaps a combination of both.

She climbed into her car and started the engine before fastening her seat belt.

Looking over her shoulder, she gave a brief wave and started down the drive before remembering the gates. Then she shrugged. Nick would remember she needed them to be opened.

It had been a peculiar day. And one she wouldn't be at all sorry to leave behind. She only hoped, for Rosie's sake, that Nick would take the initiative and call Izzy. She couldn't bear to think he'd leave his daughter so lonely and isolated.

CHAPTER SIX

WENDY BENNINGTON sat ensconced in a high-backed chair positioned so she had a view of the sweeping lawn on the west side of Fenton Hall, her injured ankle elevated on a high footstool. 'I like that girl,' she said decidedly, watching Isabel Stanford's battered car disappear down the drive. 'Talks a lot of sense. Wouldn't believe she'd ever taken an overdose, would you?'

Nick certainly wouldn't have believed it.

'She seems tougher than that,' Wendy added, accepting the cup of tea her godson handed her.

Nick absent-mindedly picked up his own teacup. It would seem that his much vaunted ability to judge character had been at fault—once again. Isabel Stanford certainly didn't blame her sister in any way. He'd misread the situation entirely.

'Pass me a digestive biscuit,' Wendy said, pointing at the plate.

Nick picked it up and held it out to her.

'Thank you,' she said, proceeding to dip the chocolate-coated biscuit in the hot liquid. 'You know, this is one of the greatest pleasures of being my age. I no longer care whether anyone thinks this is good manners or not.'

'Did you ever?' Nick was rewarded with a sniff that he knew meant that his godmother agreed.

She fixed her eyes on him. 'You're very quiet. What did you make of what Isabel had to say?'

Nick stretched out his legs. 'I think she's right in thinking a deaf unit will suit Rosie.'

'What about the girl she mentioned? Rachel? Very young, of course, but if she signs it might make Rosie feel more settled here.'

Nick didn't answer.

'You do need to do something, Nick. Rosie's devastated by her grandma's death. It might help to have someone to sign with. She certainly liked talking to Isabel.' Wendy's face grew hard. 'Ana should be horse-whipped for not having dealt with it better.'

He didn't disagree. When Rosie had finally believed what he'd told her about her grandma she'd sobbed as though her world had ended. It had ripped him in two to think that, as far as she was concerned, it probably had. She'd lost the one person she seemed to have loved, had been uprooted from the only home she'd ever known and dumped with a father she barely knew.

Nick picked up a biscuit. 'It's certainly worth meeting Rachel, particularly if she'd be prepared to act as Rosie's communicator at school.'

Wendy watched him for a moment and then sipped her tea. 'I don't think I've ever been told before that children who have cochlear implants have to learn how to interpret what they're hearing. It's fascinating.'

'That's never been an option for Rosie.'

'No,' Wendy agreed, adding, 'but it made me wonder, if Rosie had been a suitable candidate for one, how Ana would have coped with the discovery that it wasn't a cure-all.'

Nick frowned. His imagination hadn't taken him that far, but Wendy was right. Ana thought hearing aids, in whatever colour, were simply ugly. In her mind a cochlear implant would have returned Rosie to normal.

'Can't see her liking a plastic disc stuck on her daughter's head any more than she likes things attached to her ears.'

'No,' Nick agreed. She wouldn't have liked it and it would have been impossible for Rosie not to have known.

His ex-wife lived her life in a way that placed beauty beyond anything else in importance. She hated poverty and illness in equal measure. Anything Ana perceived as ugly almost caused her physical pain. It had taken him a while to see that. Even longer to realise it extended as far as their child.

He might never be able to quite forgive himself for having not fought harder to keep a relationship going with his daughter, but now, given this second chance, he wouldn't fail her.

There was so much to absorb in what Isabel had said. The idea that there was an established deaf culture was completely new to him. He hadn't known that many deaf people didn't consider themselves disabled, but described themselves as a minority group. Isabel had said that her father had passionately believed that.

He was Lydia's father too. No wonder she'd been so angry that Rosie was being denied access to her first language. He wished he'd taken the opportunity to ask more questions, had tried to understand more.

If he'd known then that Isabel had really supported her sister's actions he might have listened.

He might even have kissed her, a quiet voice whispered inside his head. There'd been moments during that dinner when he'd wanted to. He'd hated the way his body responded to her laugh and the movement of her hand through her hair. He'd not understood how he could be so attracted to a woman whose value system he completely disagreed with. After Ana, he'd vowed he would never let that happen again. And it had been easy…until Lydia.

It didn't matter. Whatever Lydia Stanford was or wasn't, Rosie had to be his priority now. But he couldn't help but wish he'd handled dinner with Lydia differently. He'd been rude—and there never was an excuse for that.

Lydia approached Fenton Hall with a sense of *déjà vu*. Almost two weeks and she hadn't given the place a thought other than to wonder how Rosie might be faring.

Actually, that was completely untrue. She'd been itching to know whether Rosie had tried to run away again, whether Sophie was still there, whether Nick had taken on board anything she'd said to him over that disastrous dinner.

Not that she'd thought it remotely likely when she'd left, although there'd been a glimmer of hope that something she'd said might have made a difference when Izzy had rung to say that Nick had called her.

Lydia rounded the final bend. The flowers he'd sent her were a nice touch too. Twenty-four long-stemmed red roses with a white card attached saying simply 'Thank you. Nick'. It was difficult not to be impressed.

She'd told herself red roses were a predicta-ble choice of flower and that twenty-four was an obscene number to send anyone. But then she'd already ascertained that he was a traditional sort of man and they habitually lacked imagination. Besides, he had plenty of money and she had given up a whole day waiting for a cat.

The heady scent of roses had filled her flat for all of last week and every time she'd looked at them she'd thought of him. Had wondered how he was getting on with Rosie. Whether his daughter was happy.

And she should have rung to say thank you for them. She'd almost done it—twice—but, for some reason, hadn't. That part annoyed her. She'd been struck down by a kind of adolescent nervousness she thought she'd long since outgrown.

Lydia pulled into the lay-by and reached over for her mobile. It was easier to phone to get the gates opened than to get out of the car and use the intercom. She always hated those things anyway. She felt so foolish talking to a crackling voice through a metal box.

Nick's card was still tucked in the front of her handbag. Her fingers hesitated before keying in the number.

She was nervous. How ridiculous.

It was probably because she'd not contacted him about the roses. She should have done that. If she saw Nick today—and she probably wouldn't—she only had to thank him for the flowers and move on. She was here to see Wendy. This was really no big deal. There was no need to feel embarrassed or remotely uncomfortable, she reminded herself sternly.

Besides, he was very unlikely to mention her leaving their dinner so precipitately because… well, why would he? Lydia bit down on her lip. The trouble was she'd been so affected by meeting Rosie that she'd forgotten there was no reason on earth why Nick should confide in her. And, if she was honest, it had hurt her that he hadn't chosen to.

'Just phone,' she said out loud. 'Get it over with. This is work.'

Obediently her fingers tapped out the number. She didn't realise how tensely she was holding herself until Christine Pearman's contained voice answered.

Her initial relief was immediately followed

by a wave of disappointment that it hadn't been Nick. Lydia stamped down hard on it. *What was the matter with her?*

'Is that Christine Pearman?' she asked, trying to inject her voice with professional confidence.

'Yes.'

'Hello. It's Lydia Stanford. Can you open the gates for me? I'm a little early, but I've got an appointment to see Wendy Bennington.'

'Yes, of course, Ms Stanford.'

Lydia tossed the mobile back onto the passenger seat and the gates started to swing open. She was almost at the house before she remembered she hadn't called back to tell Christine she was safely through. Presumably the housekeeper would have shut them anyway. She'd have to check, though. *How embarrassing.*

One glance up at the house made her feel infinitely worse. It seemed she was going to have to confront Nick after all. He was walking down the wide steps towards her. One glimpse of his athletic physique and she felt distinctly more flustered than before.

Which was illogical. Completely, utterly, irritatingly illogical. She absolutely wasn't interested in a man who hadn't been bothered to learn to sign for his daughter—even if he did fill a pair of jeans better than most.

She pulled the car to a stop and Nick was there to open the door before she'd even taken the key out of the ignition. Her voice sounded pitifully breathless as she looked up at him. 'I forgot to ring back and say I was through the gates.'

For a moment he looked confused and then he said slowly, 'They're on a timer.'

His reply left her feeling as foolish as she had when he'd calmly opened Wendy Bennington's cottage door. Of course, then she'd been standing on his godmother's roof, which had put her at a distinct disadvantage. 'Last time I was here I had to let Christine know when I was through.'

'Did you?' he asked, as though he hadn't the faintest idea why that had happened.

Lydia could feel the start of a blush. 'I suppose that might have been because Rosie had run away.' She forced herself to stop rambling and hid her face by reaching for her briefcase. 'How is she?'

'Judge for yourself,' he said, looking over his shoulder.

Behind him, Rosie was running down the steps towards her. Lydia let her briefcase fall back on the passenger seat and climbed out of the car to meet her.

Rosie's brown eyes were sparkling as she waved her hello, but what really touched Lydia was the confident way she tucked her hand inside her father's. She was so different from the stiff and awkward little girl Lydia had coaxed back to the house barely two weeks earlier.

The little girl tugged at Lydia's soft cotton skirt, waiting until she had her full attention before she signed excitedly that she had a surprise. Her young face was happy and her hands moved rapidly.

Lydia looked to Nick for confirmation that she'd properly understood what his daughter was saying. It seemed impossible that anything could have happened so quickly. 'She's got a new nanny?'

He looked at his daughter and then at Lydia. 'How can you possibly know she said that? What's the sign for nanny?'

Lydia smiled. 'Literally she signed "new person keep safe me".' Her hands moved so that Rosie was included.

Nick stroked his daughter's hair. 'I'm never going to get this.'

It was incredible—and very wonderful—to hear that he wanted to. Before Lydia could think of anything to say, she saw someone she vaguely recognised coming down the stairs.

Rachel. She pulled the name out of the recesses of her memory.

'Rachel?' *It couldn't be.* 'What are you doing here?' Lydia moved forward and lightly kissed Rachel on the cheek, standing back to look at her. The last time she'd seen her she'd had braces on her teeth.

'I'm here to support Rosie,' Rachel said, her hands moving smoothly in perfect sign language.

Everything started to fall into place. Izzy had said she knew someone who might be perfect if Nick needed someone for sign support who liked children, rather than a trained nanny.

'I'm studying for my interpreters' qualification at the moment,' Rachel said, with a swift smile at Rosie, 'and Rosie is helping me practise.'

'That's…so good.'

Rosie nodded vigorously and signed that Rachel was also teaching Daddy.

Lydia turned to look at him, her eyes wide with amazement. 'You're learning sign language?'

Nick made a really good attempt at the sign for 'try'. Rosie laughed and Rachel smiled and signed that he'd done well. Lydia felt like she'd stepped into an alternative universe. Completely different…but truly wonderful.

Tapping Rosie on the shoulder, Rachel said, 'We need to go. Rosie has a swimming lesson in half an hour.' Rosie followed the signs and flung her arms about Nick before waving goodbye to Lydia.

Lydia watched them walk round to the garages at the side of the house, her embarrassment gone. She felt a sense of satisfaction which was completely out of proportion to her contribution. 'They look like firm friends.'

'And Rachel's only been with us for a couple of days.'

'That's fantastic!'

'It couldn't have worked out better,' Nick agreed. He glanced down at his watch. 'I know you've got an appointment with Wendy, but I'm afraid she's asleep. I could wake her, but she had a bad night and you'll probably find your time is more productive if she's rested.'

'Of course.' Lydia flicked back her hair. 'Look, I could go and have a look round the shops and come back in…an hour or so. It's not a problem.'

Nick shook his head. 'Bring your briefcase inside and have a drink. Unless you need to go somewhere?' he added as an afterthought.

'A drink would be nice. It's been a long drive.' And she smiled, flicking back her hair again as it blew over her face. He was making this very easy. It was almost as though they'd parted friends and she was determined to meet him halfway. 'The traffic out of London was horrendous. I don't know where the world has decided to go today, but they're all on the motorway.'

She pulled her briefcase from the car and picked up her jacket. 'If you're busy, don't feel you have to entertain me. You can sit me somewhere and I'll work quietly on my laptop.'

Nick didn't answer straight away. He waited while she slammed the car door shut and then led the way up the steps. 'Wendy says you've made a start on the biography.'

'The publisher gave me an outline of what they particularly wanted to include and I've added some of my own ideas and roughly planned it out. It's early stages. I thought I'd talk to Wendy and see whether she feels there's anything I've missed or, conversely, something she'd prefer I left out.'

She was babbling. Lydia took a deep breath and made a mental promise that she wouldn't speak again until she'd counted to at least twenty.

'Hot or cold?'

'I beg your pardon?' Lydia said, following behind him.

'Would you prefer a hot or cold drink?'

Lydia mentally caught up. 'Cold, I think.

Thank you.' And then she remembered. 'I'd meant to say earlier, but…thank you for the flowers. I should have phoned—'

'You're welcome.'

'You didn't have to do that. I wasn't expecting…' She broke off and started again, saying simply, 'They're beautiful. Thank you.' Lydia groaned inwardly. That 'thank you' had sounded much better when she'd rehearsed it in the car. She was supposed to be back in professional mode. Cool, calm, collected and only interested in the biography she was writing.

'Wednesday is Christine's day off,' Nick remarked, pushing open the door to the kitchen.

Lydia followed. 'So you're in charge?'

'Still pampered,' he returned, with a glint of humour in his dark eyes. 'Food is left in the fridge with a stick-it note on the door telling me how long to cook it for.'

Nick opened the fridge door and Lydia caught the fluorescent yellow paper as it blew off. 'Better not lose this then,' she said, handing it back, 'or you'll be going hungry.'

He stuck it back on the front. 'You wouldn't

believe that I managed to feed myself perfectly well when I was at university.'

Lydia tucked her briefcase down beside the wall. 'I bet the quality was slightly different.'

She was surprised by that sudden smile. It had the same kick as a neat Scotch. 'I was famed for my unusual combinations.'

'Such as?'

'Have you ever tried spaghetti and cold pilchards?'

Lydia laughed. 'Fortunately not.'

'You don't know what you're missing.' Nick turned back to look at her. 'I have fresh orange. Water, obviously. Homemade lemonade…'

'Homemade lemonade would be lovely. I don't think I've ever had that before.' Lydia shifted her weight from one leg to the other. She'd forgotten quite how sexy he was. Or had she? It explained her almost breathless excitement about coming here today. Nor was she quite sure how he could make a simple T-shirt look quite so…

Well, so.

She blew her hair out of her eyes. Every

movement he made stretched the fabric over a taut male body.

'I can't take the credit for it. Christine makes it from her grandmother's recipe. The exact combination of lemons to sugar is a closely guarded secret.' He poured it into a glass and handed it to her. 'What do you think?'

Lydia took a sip. 'It's lovely.'

Nick smiled and poured himself a glass. Lydia was as beautiful as he remembered, but softer looking. Her white floating skirt finished just above her ankles and a wide belt wrapped low around her waist. The colours in the plaited leather picked out the tawny gold and rich copper threads in her hair and the warm caramel of her jacket.

He glanced down at the Anastasia Wilson jacket she held protectively in front of her. She seemed surgically attached to the blasted thing. Presumably it was this season's must-buy. 'Shall I hang that up for you?'

'Thank you.' She passed it across.

Nick carried the visual reminder of his ex-wife out into the hall and realised that, for perhaps the first time since Ana had left, he could be reminded of her and feel absolutely nothing. It was as though the angst he'd carried with him for the past four years had evaporated.

Standing there, in his hallway, he knew with complete certainty that he'd come away with the best part of their marriage—Rosie.

He slipped Lydia's jacket on to a hanger feeling euphoric. He had Rosie. What else mattered? And then he realised something else. Women didn't wear Anastasia Wilson if they knew there was a possibility of meeting him. It might mean nothing, but…

He frowned. In his experience they just didn't do that. Ana's designs were so completely distinctive. They were instantly recognisable and, since he was feeling charitable, he'd admit they were beautiful. She'd a flare for cutting fabric that sent women flocking to her when they wanted something understated yet memorable.

But women didn't wear them round him. Not if they knew she was his ex-wife. It seemed to be some unwritten code. As though to do so would be rubbing salt into a wound. Which meant that Lydia still didn't know…

And that meant she hadn't gone home looking for the 'skeleton in the closet'. A concentrated search would have found considerably more information on him than she'd brought up by typing in 'Nick Regan'. She'd have been able to read about the man Ana had left him for. Handsome, French, well-connected and one of his oldest friends.

She'd have known that their affair hadn't lasted long. Ana had made the contacts she'd needed, became bored and returned to London. By the time their divorce was final she'd moved back to Hampstead Heath and billionaire Simon Cameron had taken up residence in the former marital home.

Was it really possible she still didn't know?

CHAPTER SEVEN

NICK walked slowly back into the kitchen. He felt as if the ground had started shifting beneath his feet, so much so that he wasn't sure what he believed about anything any more.

Lydia hadn't moved. Her back rested on the central island unit and she was sipping her lemonade. Was it really possible that her interest was focused exactly where she said it was—exclusively on Wendy Bennington?

If so, the irony was that he probably knew more about her than she did about him.

He knew Lydia had never been married, but had been romantically linked to at least two high profile men. That she'd graduated from Cambridge six years after he'd left there himself and that her career trajectory had had the forward motion of an arrow in flight. In fact, every indication was that she was a serious-minded journalist who took what she did very seriously indeed.

Which was why his godmother had wanted her as her biographer, that small inner voice reminded him. More specifically, Wendy had wanted her because of an article Lydia had written on Third World famine. She'd described it as 'insightful' and a 'bloody sight more interesting than many things I've read on the subject'.

Nick felt like a fool.

He'd been adamant that journalists were the scum of the earth on the grounds that he had the emotional scarring to prove it. Wendy had argued that, as in all professions, there were good and bad. Bad journalists chased a 'story' in the hope of building their own reputations; good journalists wanted to change the world.

He hadn't listened. Hadn't been prepared to. He'd been so convinced that Lydia had orchestrated the Steven Daly trial for her own benefit that he'd filtered everything so it supported that belief. He couldn't deny she'd written some life

changing stories, but each one had systematically built her career. Her piece on Third World
famine had won her a prestigious award. He'd
never questioned her ability, only her motivation.

He'd argued that if Lydia was the kind of journalist who would use her own sister's private
grief, what would stop her from using his? If her
primary aim was to find things out that no one
knew and publish them before anyone else, then
Ana's rejection of Rosie would make interesting copy. It would even be possible to make it
sound as though she was championing people
whom society considered outside the 'norm'.

But Lydia hadn't done any kind of search on him.

'Shall we take our drinks outside?'

Lydia hesitated. 'Don't you have things you
need to be doing? I really don't want to get in the
way.'

'I'm ready for a break and it's a beautiful temperature now. I suspect it's going to be too hot
to be out there later.'

'You're sure you've got the time?'

Nick nodded and ushered her through the

sunroom and on to the terrace. As the sunshine hit her face Nick heard Lydia's small purr of pleasure and he felt something inside him splinter.

Whatever it was that had kept him cocooned and protected had shattered. It left him feeling vulnerable, like an old-time knight without his armour.

And he wasn't sorry. There was danger in this—and excitement. It was like starting out on an adventure without having any idea what the outcome would be. He couldn't remember the last time he'd been reckless in his private life.

Nick led her across to the comfortable Lloyd Loom chairs with their white calico cushions and watched her settle into one.

'It's beautiful here,' she said softly and glanced across at him.

He didn't quite have time to look away and her eyebrows rose in a mute question. Nick shook his head, uncertain what to say. Or even where to begin.

'What happened to Sophie in the end?' Lydia

asked, her hands cradled around the coldness of her tumbler.

'She decided she didn't like working outside London, so we mutually decided to waive the notice period.'

Lydia laughed. 'How…convenient.'

'Wasn't it?' he agreed easily. It was a miracle his voice sounded so steady. He felt as if the world had started spinning on a different axis.

Lydia took a sip of her lemonade. 'Did Rosie's mother mind you arbitrarily removing her choice of nanny?' And then she slapped a hand over her mouth and shook her head. 'I'm sorry. I was so determined I wouldn't ask those kinds of questions.'

'It doesn't matter.'

'I—'

Nick interrupted her. 'Lydia, I owe you an apology for the other night.' He needed to give more. 'I was very rude to you—and you didn't deserve that. I…appreciate your concern for Rosie.'

Her eyes widened slightly and then she half shook her head. 'You would probably have got there without my meddling. I shouldn't be so quick to give my opinions. It really wasn't my business to—'

'And, in answer to your question, I haven't asked her.' His index finger swept a clear line through the condensation on his glass. 'Ana is…more than happy to delegate.'

Lydia turned to look at him and he was almost certain she'd understood exactly what he'd wanted to convey. There was a momentary flash of sympathy, for him or Rosie he didn't know, and then she made a determined effort to lighten the atmosphere.

She set her empty glass down on the low table. 'Rachel is lovely. I used to be her babysitter. Did she tell you?'

Nick nodded. 'And that her parents are profoundly deaf.'

'They were close friends of my parents.' Lydia twisted one strand of hair in a small corkscrew on her finger. 'We used to go on holidays together. Once we hired a narrowboat and went up the Grand Union Canal…' She smiled. 'They live a couple of streets away from my aunt and uncle, so even after Mum and Dad died they kept a close eye on Izzy. Made sure she was doing all right.'

'Whereas you went to university?'

Lydia looked up. 'Yes. Yes, I did.'

It took a moment before she realised that he probably hadn't meant that the way it had sounded to her. He'd stated simple fact. Izzy had gone to live with relatives and she'd gone to university. It was the truth.

Lydia wiggled her left foot out of her sandal and watched the sunlight glint on the intricate gold toe ring. Nick couldn't know the guilt she still felt over that decision. No one knew. It was something she carried deep within herself.

It was her own private burden to know that if she'd made a different choice then it was possible she'd have been able to prevent Steven Daly ever becoming important in her sister's life. She had to live with the knowledge that she'd selfishly ploughed on with her original plans.

In the beginning it had been easy. She'd told herself her parents wouldn't have wanted her to do anything else. That she'd worked hard for her place at Cambridge, the only person from her state school to be offered one, and they wouldn't have wanted her to give it up. She'd consoled herself with the thought that Izzy would be fine with Auntie Margaret.

But Izzy had cried. Had begged her. Twelve years old and she'd wanted to stay in her home. And it would have been possible—if Lydia had assumed the responsibility of being her legal guardian.

Everyone had made it very easy. Auntie Margaret and her family were only too happy to take Izzy in. They'd decorated a bedroom especially for her and had carefully transferred all her sister's posters so she would feel at home.

Only Lydia knew that she was too selfish ever to have given up her dream. She'd consoled herself with the thought that her future success would justify that decision. The need to prove her decision had been the right one had been the driving force of her life.

'What made you decide on being a journalist?' His voice startled her.

Lydia glanced up, glad to be pulled away from memories that hurt. She chewed gently on the side of her mouth as she considered her answer. 'Does it sound too pretentious to say I wanted to make a difference?'

Her smile was almost shy. Nick watched as she pleated the soft cotton of her skirt. 'No.' His answer surprised him. *Amazingly, no.*

'I decided I didn't have the temperament of a saint,' she continued, her smile self-derisory, 'so I had to find a different route. I was hopelessly naïve.'

He waited for her to say more, and when she didn't he prompted, 'Journalism isn't what you hoped for?'

'Human nature isn't.' She gave him a swift smile. 'It's painful sometimes to stand dispassionately on the sidelines reporting what you're seeing, but doing nothing to actually stop it. I have a natural tendency to want to fix everything and it's not always possible.'

'Not always,' Nick murmured in agreement.

An expression of sadness moved over her face like ripples in a puddle. If he'd been Wendy it would have prompted him to ask Lydia about Izzy's overdose and everything surrounding it—but he couldn't bring himself to intrude into what must be a deeply private place.

Or perhaps he wasn't that noble, merely scared of Lydia's reaction. Trust was something that was earned and he'd offered little by way of fair exchange.

'Have you ever regretted it?'

She smiled. 'Many times. When you say you want to be a journalist everyone warns you you'll start by doing the obituaries.' Her smile widened and the result was infectious. 'That's not far from the truth, although in my case I wrote the "What's On" pages for the local *Herald*. Equally dull and certainly not what I'd planned to be writing about.'

'But you didn't have to wait long for your big break.'

'No.'

'You must have been very young when you went to work undercover in a care home,' he prompted, wanting to know more about her.

'They wanted someone who wouldn't be suspected, so I posed as a student needing holiday work. What I saw was shocking…' She broke off. 'How do you know about that?'

He'd spoken without thinking. Nick felt as though the world had stilled around him and only the two of them were left moving. He decided on honesty. 'I looked you up.'

'You looked me up?' she echoed.

He shrugged, half nonchalant, half apologetic. 'I know you've a first in English and Politics from Cambridge, that your first job was on a local paper in Manchester, that your professed hobbies include hang-gliding and the theatre.'

There was silence while she assimilated what he'd told her.

'Actually,' she said slowly, 'I don't like hang-gliding.'

He hadn't expected that reaction. 'You don't?'

Lydia smiled. 'You can't believe everything you read.' Her lips twitched with suppressed laughter. 'I was asked to do an on camera report about hang-gliding and I couldn't do it. First time ever I'd bottled out of a job, but I'm totally scared of heights. It didn't matter how safe they tried to convince me it was.' Then she looked across at him, her incredible eyes full of mischief. 'So you looked me up?'

'Yes.'

'Did you find the bit about the award I won?'

'On the issues surrounding Third World famine? Yes.'

And then she laughed. She turned her sparkling eyes on him to ask, 'Was it just idle curiosity or were you looking for something specific?'

Nick knew he'd been right not to relax. 'Honestly?'

'Of course.'

He hadn't really expected any other answer from her. Not now. 'I was looking for something that would convince Wendy to reject you as her biographer.'

The laughter disappeared from those amber depths and he almost wished the words unsaid. 'Why?'

He looked down at his hands and then back at her expectant face. Honesty deserved honesty.

'I remembered your name from the Steven Daly court case.'

'Many people do,' she said quietly.

'I believed you were driven by ambition rather than…a sense of justice and…'

'Go on.' Her voice had a steely edge to it.

'And there's not much more to say. I thought you'd seen an opportunity and gone for it.'

Lydia sat back in her seat. His words had shocked her but, strangely, they hadn't surprised her. They explained so much. 'You thought I'd put Izzy through that…for me.'

'Yes.' He met her gaze unflinchingly. She had to admire him for that.

She let out her breath on a hiss. She'd wondered why he'd been so antagonistic towards her. Now she knew. His attitude towards her had seemed so unreasonable—but if he'd seriously believed she'd been capable of using her sister's situation to build her career it made complete sense.

Lydia shook her head. 'I would never do that.' She was guilty of many things, but not that. 'Why did you think I'd do that?'

Nick leant forward in his chair, his elbows resting on his knees. 'It was the way Isabel looked during the trial.'

She nodded. She could understand that. Izzy had been frightened and intimidated by the whole experience.

'And then she disappeared from view.'

'She was exhausted,' Lydia said quietly.

'Not surprisingly, now I think about it objectively.' Nick pulled a hand through his hair. 'But at the time… *Hell!* I don't know what I was thinking exactly. I suppose I thought that, although Steven Daly was convicted on all counts of embezzlement and fraud, the only real winner seemed to be you.'

Lydia felt as if she'd been doused in ice-cold water. She'd never thought it could be seen from that perspective. She wanted to cry out that it was unfair, palpably untrue—and then she thought of the opportunities that had come her way because the case had been given such a high profile.

Steven Daly had been a tiny cog in a much larger machine. As she'd picked away at why he'd needed a quick injection of cash she'd uncovered a trail of deceit and fraudulent business practices. Lydia had followed every lead tenaciously, she'd called in favours from friends and used every skill she possessed to bring down an insurance scam far bigger than anything she'd dreamed of.

And what had Izzy got out of it? Nothing but the intrusive sympathy of strangers.

Whereas she…

Nick's voice was low. 'When I met her last week it was immediately obvious I'd misread the situation completely. I'm very sorry.'

Which explained the roses.

Lydia looked across at him earnestly leaning forward, his elbows resting on his knees. He might have misread the situation in thinking she'd forced Izzy through the court case to further her career, but he was right in thinking that she hadn't acted on her sister's behalf.

The truth of that had been nagging at the back of her mind for the past couple of years. She forced her foot back into her sandal. 'No, you're right. I did it for me.'

His head snapped up. She hated the look of surprise on his face. It would be easier to accept his apology and move on, but that wouldn't be fair—either to him or Izzy—and it wouldn't be the truth.

'I don't think I fully realised it at the time, but it was my revenge, not hers. When I began, Izzy wasn't in any condition to give an opinion on it and, if I'm honest—' she looked out across the lawn '—I'm not sure I'd have asked her anyway. I hated Steven Daly and I didn't even know one tenth of what he was guilty of. I'd no idea he'd stolen from anyone but Izzy.'

Nick sat silent and she appreciated that. Few people, if any, had ever allowed her to express how much she'd hated Izzy's ex-boyfriend for what he'd done to her sister.

Hate was ugly. Hate gnawed away at you and destroyed you. She knew that, but hate had been her motivation. The charitable would say it was love for her sister, but she hadn't acted out of love. It had been a desire for vengeance, and vengeance hadn't healed Izzy.

Time had. Time and the self-worth her parents

had instilled within her with years of loving. That had been the panacea. It had nothing to do with Lydia's meticulously researched investigation into her ex-boyfriend's business practices.

Slowly, painfully slowly, Izzy had rebuilt her life because she'd found the inner strength to do it. It had all taken so long. Nothing had happened with the speed Lydia had wanted and she'd been glad she'd had another focus for her energy.

Izzy had made great strides forward only to slip back. It had been excruciating to watch but, over time, there'd gradually been more good days than bad. The loss of the man who'd lied and stolen from her was separated out from the miscarriage of her baby. With counselling she'd come to see them as different issues.

Izzy had needed time and space to grieve for the loss of her baby. Knowing she was carrying a new life had been the only thing she'd had to console her when her world had crashed around her ears—and it had been the final loss, the one she'd been unable to cope with.

'She certainly doesn't blame you.'

Lydia looked up, wanting him to understand. 'I find that quite difficult to deal with because you're right. She did hate the court case and I made her do it because Steven Daly was— is—' she corrected herself '—a truly foul man.'

'Many hundreds of people lost their life savings because of him,' Nick said quietly.

'I'm not sure Izzy was in any place to really care.' Lydia twisted the fronds of her belt into a tight screw and watched them slowly unravel. 'The thing she found most difficult was having to stand up in court and face him. I'm certain she wouldn't have done it…' *Without me*, she finished silently, aware that if she tried to say those words out loud her voice would have cracked.

She knew that Izzy would have buckled under the pressure if she hadn't been there to propel her through the whole experience by the full force of her personality. *Her* sense of justice. *Her* need to see him suffer.

At eighteen she hadn't been prepared to stay and look after Izzy. She'd felt she'd failed her and was determined not to fail her again. She hadn't stopped to think whether it was what Izzy wanted.

She looked up. 'I couldn't bear it that he should get away with everything. So you were right…in a way. It was about me. Izzy is too gentle a person to think about revenge or punishment.'

Nick felt the slow burning of an almost incandescent anger towards the man who had hurt these women so much. If Steven Daly hadn't already been safely behind bars he might have been tempted to see what he could do.

How could he have misjudged Lydia so much? Nick watched the pain pass across her face and wished he could do something to make it all go away. There was nothing. She'd said it herself—time was the only thing that could heal hurt like that.

Perhaps the only thing he could do for her was not offer platitudes and spurious comments of sympathy.

Nick cleared his throat. 'Do you want to walk?' As she looked up, her face unusually vulnerable, he felt his smile twist. 'Wendy will wonder what I've done to you.'

She gave a half laugh and swiped at her eyes. 'Do I look a mess?'

'You look beautiful.'

He'd spoken without thinking and his voice resonated with honesty. He saw her eyes widen and then she said quietly, 'A walk would be nice.'

'I'll take you to inspect my kitchen garden.' Nick stood up and held out his hand. In the heartbeat before she allowed him to pull her up from the chair he wondered whether he should have done it.

As his fingers closed around hers he wondered what would happen if he pulled her in close and held her…for comfort. Only for comfort. She was so close he could smell the soft scent of her perfume.

Instead he let go of her hand and turned to face the sweeping west lawn. Lydia walked beside him. Every so often he felt the soft flick of her hair as it was blown against his bare arm. Once he glanced down to see if she'd noticed, but her eyes were fixed on a weeping willow in the distance. She was staring at the cascade of delicate lance-shaped leaves as though she'd never seen anything so fascinating.

Nick wanted to say something that would help her, something that would soften that hard edge of guilt. He settled on a quiet, 'Knowing Steven Daly is in prison must have helped your sister's recovery.'

Lydia turned to look at him, the soft breeze catching her hair and blowing it across her face. She raised a shaking hand and pushed it back. 'I'm not sure it makes any difference to Izzy.' And then she thought and added, 'Perhaps. A little. Maybe knowing she isn't about to turn a corner and walk into him has allowed her to heal, but…' she shook her head '…he isn't in prison because of anything he did to her.'

Lydia didn't dare blink. Tears pricked hard behind her eyes and she felt as though a hard lump had settled in her throat. 'I just can't get my head round that. Where is the justice in someone being able to deliberately wreck another person's life and there be no redress?'

'There isn't any.'

Lydia took a deep shaking breath. 'Izzy voluntarily transferred the money from the sale of our parents' house into a joint bank account. So if he hadn't used the money to shield his illegal activities from detection I wouldn't have been able to touch him. It made no difference to anyone that Steven is a vicious bully.'

'Physically?'

Lydia smiled, but it was entirely without humour. 'If he'd touched her physically I would have got to him long before I did. Domestic violence is a crime. There are laws in place to protect women from that.'

'But nothing to stop him stealing an inheritance.'

'His legal representatives argued very convincingly that there was no theft involved.' Even now, after two years, that hurt. 'It made no difference that he'd systematically set about breaking Izzy until she would do practically anything he asked her to do. We didn't have any proof, so that was that.'

'Did you know what was happening at the time?' he asked quietly.

Lydia nodded. 'Living away in London, it meant I saw the changes in her quite clearly. Over time she lost her sparkle. She began to change the way she dressed, stopped meeting her friends… Hundreds of little things that in themselves didn't mean anything, but when you started to put them together they became much more sinister.'

'Wasn't there anything you could do?'

Lydia shrugged. Nick's questions came in a calm, matter-of-fact voice that made it easy to answer him. *At the time there'd been nothing she could do.* Though it hurt to remember that. 'Izzy loved him. Or thought she did.' She wrapped a protective arm around her waist. 'He could be very charming when he chose to be. Do you know the kind of man I mean?'

Nick thought about some of the corporate bullies he'd met. The smoothly manipulative ones who would act as though they were your best friend before stabbing you in the back at the first opportunity. He nodded.

'Of course when I first met him I didn't know anything about his business dealings; I only knew I didn't like him.' She smiled that tense, humourless smile again. 'He didn't like me either, but I can't blame him for that. From the very beginning I was doing everything I could to undermine him. I advised Izzy not to live with him, not to have a joint bank account, certainly not to have a family with him.'

'Did he know that?'

'I imagine so. She told him everything.' She gave a sigh and continued, 'He managed to convince Izzy I was jealous of him—and of their happiness. I'd finished a fairly serious relationship about that time. It all sounded plausible enough.'

'Except you knew you weren't jealous.'

Lydia looked up and smiled. 'Hindsight is a wonderful thing. I don't even know I knew that for certain. I may well not have liked anyone Izzy became so intensely involved with so young.' She paused. 'Though, to be fair to me, I specifically hated the pressure he put on her to sell our parents' house.'

'Surely you needed to agree to that?' *If the house had been left to them jointly?* It must have been left in trust while Isabel had been a minor. His mind started to think of everything that should have protected a vulnerable girl from becoming a target of a predator like Daly.

Her voice broke in on his thoughts, unusually toneless and edged with pain. 'I didn't have much choice. Izzy was nineteen by then and Steven convinced her they needed the money for their future. I dragged everything out as long as I could. I "forgot" to give the tenants notice, I insisted on marketing the house at too high a price...'

Nick smiled. It was easy to imagine Lydia doing that. 'He must have hated you.'

'He had his revenge. He used it as an opportunity to drive a wedge between Izzy and me.'

'I can't see that working. She idolises you.'

'Now.' She shook her head. 'Not then. Izzy was twelve when our parents died and she went to live with my mother's sister and her family. I went to university. We hadn't shared a house for six years by the time Steven came on the scene. It wasn't as difficult as you might think for him to insinuate himself into her life.'

She reached out and brushed away an angry tear. 'Anyway, the house eventually sold and Izzy's share of the money was transferred to her account. It took a few months longer for him to persuade her to put everything in joint names.'

'And then he emptied the account.'

'Basically.' Lydia rubbed her hand along her arm as though she suddenly felt cold. It had nothing to do with the weather, which was still balmy and hot. 'Izzy didn't know and, even when she did, he managed to convince her it was a temporary business hitch. She certainly didn't tell me until weeks later, by which time he'd left her anyway.'

Another swipe at her eyes and she took a shuddering breath. 'I'm sorry. I don't know why I'm crying.'

Nick did. He would never have described himself as a particularly imaginative man, but he was having no difficulty at all in empathising with everything she was telling him. There was nothing he could do to help her but listen.

'Anyway, it was a life-changing experience. I've spent the last year or so concentrating on raising public awareness. Society needs to protect other women from men like Steven Daly.'

'It's been successful,' Nick observed quietly.

'I've worked hard. I thought I was focused before, but this has been more like a crusade. I really believe in what I'm doing. The fact that it's brought me professional respect is a by-product. I'd do it anyway.'

They walked through the narrow opening to the enclosed wall garden. Nick kept silent, instinctively knowing she wouldn't want anything else.

Lydia looked around at a kitchen garden that was still very much in the early stages of planning. He watched as her expression altered and she breathed softly. 'This is going to be amazing.'

Her eyes still held a hint of remembered pain, but she was back in control. The mask she wore to protect herself from the world was back in place. Even so, Nick didn't think he would ever be able to look at her again without remembering how vulnerable she could be. *The real Lydia Stanford.*

He looked around the kitchen garden which had taken him so many hours. It had been the place where he'd come to terms with many of his own demons. 'It's been slow going. When I arrived there was an old greenhouse on the site, which had been smashed. I've spent the better part of this year clearing away debris and picking pieces of glass out of the soil.'

Lydia's eyes followed the far wall with its fan-trained peach trees. 'It's coming along now, though.' She walked between two beds and stopped. 'I don't recognise this.'

'*Allium cepa "Prolifera".*' He smiled, watching the way she gently stroked the plant. 'It's a tree onion. I think it's the most decorative form of the onion family. The onions themselves are small but strong. Fine for pickling.'

He loved the way her eyes darted about the enclosed space. 'This is south-facing, isn't it?'

'Yes. It gets the sun for most of the day, until late in the afternoon, and the fact that it's so sheltered should make it highly productive.'

'You might be able to experiment with more exotic fruit and vegetables here.' She looked up at him and he felt his heart tighten so that he felt almost breathless. 'I must get a garden. I do miss it.'

Nick glanced down at his watch. 'We've given Wendy an hour. We ought to start heading back.'

With one last look over her shoulder, Lydia led the way out of the kitchen garden. As they left the enclosed space the summer breeze whipped at her hair. She caught it and twisted it into a loose plait.

Nick felt his stomach twist. Lydia was beautiful, intelligent and caring. It was hardly surprising that he should be attracted to her.

But a woman as vibrant as Lydia Stanford was never going to be interested in a man like him. A single father, tied to one place in one country. No adventures. No great causes.

They walked back across the lawn towards the house. What he needed to do was let Lydia get on with her job. She was here to see Wendy.

He had to remember that when she'd gathered all the information she needed she'd be gone.

CHAPTER EIGHT

NEVER cry all over a man—they don't like it. Who had said that? Lydia returned with the tray of filter coffee and mugs and set it down on a low table.

She couldn't remember who'd given such sage advice, but she wished she'd paid more attention to it. Her third visit within eight days to Fenton Hall and Nick was noticeable by his absence. When she'd left after seeing Wendy the first time he'd been taking an important telephone call from Germany. On her second visit he'd been in London. This time he was expecting a conference call and was in his study.

It *might* be coincidental that he was never around, but if she'd been a betting woman she'd have laid odds on it not being. In her opinion it was beginning to look as if her arrival was his cue to disappear and she wasn't holding her breath in expectation of seeing him before she left today. When she'd gone to ask Christine for coffee his study door had been wide open and his computer switched off, but he'd been nowhere to be seen.

She pushed down the plunger. Perhaps she'd embarrassed him by crying? Maybe it had been information overload and he'd felt uncomfortable? Certainly she shouldn't have cried. She never cried.

She hadn't meant to. It had shocked her that he'd thought she would have deliberately used Izzy…and then she'd started talking and hadn't seemed able to stop. He hadn't seemed to mind. In fact, he'd been lovely. Surprisingly so.

Something had shifted the last time she'd seen him. It had felt as if they'd reached a new understanding, had begun a friendship. She shrugged. Clearly not. He'd obviously been marking time until his godmother woke. Anything else had been in her imagination.

Wendy put the sheaf of papers she'd been reading on the small table to her side. 'Are we done for today?'

'I think so,' Lydia said, lifting the coffee jug. 'You ought to have a rest after you've drunk your coffee…and I've got plenty to be going on with.' She smiled. 'Eighty-five thousand words, to be precise.'

'You know, it's depressing to think I was talking about all this twenty years ago,' Wendy said, indicating the papers at her side. 'I read the other day that the Amazon rainforest is currently being flattened at a rate of six football pitches every day. Six! And in some remote parts there's just one forestry agent to monitor an area four times the size of Switzerland.'

Lydia poured the coffee. 'I thought governments were now committed to stopping forest-clearing.'

'There's a big difference between what a politician promises before an election and what he delivers after it,' Wendy said dryly. 'Depressing, but true. It's complicated, of course. One can only be sympathetic to a country which needs agricultural businesses to keep expanding if they're to pay their external debt, but that's why I personally believe we should remove the debt…'

'Is something the matter?' Lydia asked as Wendy trailed off, her attention claimed by something outside the window. The elderly woman's face had lost its crusading fire and had become wistful.

'It's Nick.'

Nick. Immediately Lydia's stomach did a kind of belly flop.

'In the garden.' Wendy turned her head to look at her.

Lydia carried a bone china mug over to where Wendy was sitting. It gave her a perfect view of the sweeping lawn…and Nick. Nick and Rosie.

She watched as he swung his daughter round and landed her carefully, their faces full of laughter. Father and daughter. They made a striking couple. Nick in dark blue denim jeans and an olive-green T-shirt, Rosie in yellow shorts and equally bright cotton sun-top. They could easily have been part of a television advert.

'It's good to see that relationship building,' Wendy observed from her chair. 'Give him time and I think he'll be a fine father. Better than his own, anyway. Though that's not saying much.' She sipped her coffee. 'George was a cold man.'

Lydia glanced down at the grey head, hair neatly twisted into a chignon. She longed to ask questions. Her mouth twisted. It wouldn't be wise. Wendy was sharp enough to notice and she wasn't sure yet why she was so interested in everything concerning Nick.

He might be making great strides in building a relationship with Rosie now, but the fact remained that he hadn't done much in the previous five years. When she actually thought about it, that aspect of his character wasn't attractive at all.

So why did she feel this compulsion to see him, talk to him? Maybe she was piqued by the fact that he didn't seem remotely interested in her.

'Fortunately there's enough of his mother in him to make Nick worth bothering about.'

Lydia deliberately moved away from the window. It was almost painful to see how happy Nick and Rosie were together. Beautiful to see, of course, but she felt a stab of envy as she watched them. She didn't understand why that was, either. It all smacked of domesticity and she avoided that like the plague.

'Jennifer, Nick's mother, was a lovely girl. Died when Nick was a young baby,' Wendy continued as Lydia took her own cup and sat down again on the coral-coloured sofa. 'She had rheumatic fever when she was a child and was never very strong afterwards.'

'Did Nick's father marry again?' Lydia asked, trying to keep her voice light and neutral. It seemed an innocuous enough question.

Wendy snorted as though it were the stupidest of suggestions. 'It was surprising he found anyone to marry him the first time. Complete bore of a man, though very handsome. I never liked him. Thought he knew better than anyone else on any subject. Didn't believe it was possible for a woman to understand world market indices. After thirty years of arguing with him, I finally came to the conclusion I'd leave him in his ignorance.'

Even filtering that snippet of information through an understanding of Wendy, it still gave an evocative picture of Nick's father and, by extension, his childhood.

He'd grown up without a mother. That didn't surprise her. *And with a distant father.* She was even less surprised by that. Lydia sipped her coffee and wrinkled her nose at the bitter taste. She leant forward and spooned in a teaspoon of brown sugar. 'What's happened to Rosie's mother? Has she died?'

'Ana? Dead?' Wendy smiled grimly. 'No. Why did you think that?'

Lydia sat back. 'I—I don't know. I just wondered—'

'Rosie's mother is Anastasia Wilson. She's not dead. Though she's just about as much use,' Wendy added after a moment.

Anastasia Wilson. For one moment Lydia wasn't sure she'd heard correctly.

'She's a fashion designer. Has her own label now, I believe.'

'Yes, I know,' Lydia said. 'I love her clothes, but… *Anastasia Wilson* is Rosie's mother?'

Wendy gave her habitual snort of derision. 'Well, she gave birth to her, but she hasn't done

much mothering. Left all that to her own
mother.'

'Who's just died,' Lydia said under her breath,
finally understanding why Rosie had come to
live with Nick.

Wendy didn't seem to have heard her. 'As soon
as there was the slightest possibility she might
have to assume some parental responsibility Ana
passed Rosie over to Nick.'

As though she'd been a parcel. *Poor little girl.*
No wonder she'd looked so stiff and lonely
when she'd first seen her. No one had even
bothered to tell Rosie her grandmother had died.

But...

Her mind seemed to have frozen on the one
thought—*Anastasia Wilson had been married to
Nick Regan-Phillips.* It had the same impact as
if Wendy had said he'd been married to the
Queen. It didn't seem possible.

They were two completely disparate people
with, surely, nothing in common. Lydia had
been at the same function as Anastasia Wilson
several times without actually 'meeting' her, but
she had read several articles about her in glossy

magazines. Any visit to a dentist waiting room inevitably brought you into contact with one. She didn't remember any mention of Nick or of her having a child.

She frowned as she tried to pull disregarded information into the forefront of her mind. Anastasia, she was sure, currently lived with a man who Lydia would describe as having too much of everything: too tanned, too blond and too rich. And before that there'd been…Gaston Girard, the charismatic tennis star whose family had been involved in fashion for several generations. He'd seemed a better idea, but slightly too smooth for her taste.

But, a child? She couldn't remember anything about Anastasia Wilson having a child.

Most recently it had been about her fabulous new home in Jamaica and the inspiration she'd found experiencing a new culture. There'd been some mouth-watering photographs of her last collection, soft wisps of chiffon which had been turned into stunning evening gowns.

Without a doubt, Anastasia Wilson had an incredible flare for colour and a seemingly effortless ability to make the woman in her designs shine rather than her clothes. She was a brilliant designer. In fact, one of her favourites. But as a woman…

As a woman she came across as shallow, vain and rather silly. Everything she said was peppered with anecdotes of parties, people and places.

Married to Nick Regan-Phillips?

No. She couldn't believe it. Nick was fearsomely intelligent. Quiet and private. It just didn't fit.

Lydia wanted to ask so many questions. How long were they married? How did they meet? Why did they divorce…?

And then she remembered her jacket and cringed. Had Nick recognised it as one of his ex-wife's designs? *Who was she kidding?* Of course he had. It was unmistakable.

But she hadn't known. If she'd known who his ex-wife was, she'd never have worn…

Anastasia Wilson was Rosie's mother. That single fact pounded in her head and still she couldn't quite take it in.

'I'd no idea Anastasia Wilson had any children. I'm sure I've never seen any pictures…'

Wendy shook her head sadly. 'When Rosie was a baby there were plenty of photographs of them taken together, but in recent years…no.'

Lydia frowned.

'She's deaf.' And then, because Lydia clearly hadn't made the connection, Wendy added, 'Ana has a real problem with having a deaf daughter. She strives for perfect…and deaf isn't perfect. Not for her.'

Lydia swore softly. This beggared belief. 'Who taught Rosie to sign?'

'Nick asked Ana about that the other day.' Wendy paused to readjust her leg on the footstool. 'Apparently Ana's mother was very keen on it. There's some research to show that all babies, hearing or otherwise, do better intellectually if they sign pre-language. At least that's how she sold it to Ana. Makes me think a lot better of Georgina. I'd always thought she was a fairly stupid woman for giving birth to Ana, but…'

Georgina being Rosie's grandmother, Lydia thought, trying to piece together so many new pieces of information.

'...obviously not so stupid after all. She was also the person who insisted Rosie went to a nursery school with a deaf unit.'

Thank God for Georgina. But where had Nick been in this? Why hadn't he been the one insisting on the sign language and finding nurseries?

'So Nick hasn't told you anything about Ana?'

'No.' Lydia put her empty coffee cup down on the table. *He certainly hadn't.*

'Can't blame the boy for that. He should never have married her.' Wendy finished the last of her coffee. 'Though I doubt I'd have listened to me in his position. I've never been able to see much point in any marriage. I've always thought there had to be more to life than handing round hors d'oeuvres and having babies, so I'm no judge of what will suit other people.'

She lifted her leg off the footstool and reached behind her for the crutches resting against the chair back. Lydia was on her feet but Wendy waved her away. 'Have you ever used crutches?'

'No.'

'Can't wait to get rid of the things.' Wendy started towards the door. 'We're not meeting now until next week are we?'

Lydia shook her head. 'You've got an ortho-paedic out-patient appointment tomorrow and I've got a book launch to go to the following day.'

'Until next week, then.'

Lydia resisted every impulse to help her, knowing how much that would be resented. She slowly gathered together all her papers and tucked them into her briefcase.

It really was impossible to think of anything other than the fact that Nick had been married to Anastasia Wilson. If she was being really rude, she couldn't quite get her head round the fact that an intelligent man had married a woman who talked in a 'little girl' voice.

Hadn't it grated? Or had he been completely mesmerised by her petite frame and cloud of jet-black hair? And with a spurt of jealousy she realised she didn't want to think about that.

Lydia put the final papers, the ones Wendy

had been reading, in her briefcase and clicked it shut. She looked out of the window where Nick and Rosie had been.

They'd gone.

There was just that long expanse of lawn leading down to the weeping willow and on to a tightly packed spinney. There was no chance of seeing Nick today then. It was probably for the best, but…

She felt strangely purposeless. It would have been nice to have spoken to him. Seen Rosie. Lydia glanced down at her watch and debated whether she should make the drive home or stop in Cambridge for some retail therapy. There was so much she should be doing, but she didn't have the motivation.

Even though the sunlight had shone brightly through the windows all morning, the midday sun was something of a shock when Lydia walked out on to the stone steps. Heat hit her like a wall. She wrinkled her nose as she thought of the long sticky car journey home.

She crossed the front courtyard and unlocked her car, putting her briefcase inside, as the sound of scrunching gravel made her look up. Rosie came running round the corner as a streak of yellow. She looked bright, happy and very hot.

Lydia smiled, loving to see her energy and exuberance. It was what a childhood should be about. Rosie caught sight of her and waved a hand.

Anastasia Wilson's daughter. Now she knew she could see her mother in the dark curling hair and the almond-shaped eyes. A beauty—but not perfect enough for Anastasia. Lydia felt a wave of sheer anger at the ignorance and injustice of that.

Lydia shut the car door and waited until Rosie was near enough to sign. She wanted to ask where Nick was, but settled on asking where Rosie was running to.

The little girl's eyes shone with excitement. Her hands moved to show a square rug laid out on the floor and then she peppered her picnic with strawberries and cream, cheese, bread, small cakes and, best of all, crisps. They were her favourite and she'd picked them out of the cupboard herself, four whole packets.

Lydia laughed and told her she didn't like strawberries. After a moment of surprise Rosie signed that they also had bananas, but clearly she didn't feel they were as good. *She was an absolute sweetheart.* How could her mother not love and cherish her?

She saw Nick's shadow before she saw him. He rounded the bend and stopped when he saw her. Lydia instinctively smoothed down the skirt of her layered sundress. She waited while he crossed the courtyard towards her. 'Hello.'

'Hello,' he replied. And then, 'You've finished early. I thought you wouldn't be leaving for another hour or so.'

His words sharpened the suspicion that he'd been deliberately avoiding her. For a moment that hurt—and then she looked into his eyes and caught a glimpse of something that turned everything on its head. She saw a definite flicker of desire in their hazel depths.

And then she remembered something else. He'd said she was beautiful. With sudden clarity she realised he'd meant it and now she saw it in his eyes.

So why avoid her? That part didn't make any sense. Unless he still thought she was the kind of journalist who'd sell any kind of story. *Did he still think that?* It felt very important that he shouldn't still think that.

'We're going on a picnic.' His hand rested lightly on his daughter's head.

Lydia tossed back her hair, which was lying heavily about her shoulders. 'I know.' She smiled down at Rosie. 'And you've raided Christine's cupboards and taken four packets of crisps.'

'Do you think I've over-catered?'

Lydia felt a smile tug at her lips. 'Probably not.' Small lines fanned out at the edges of his eyes. *Gorgeous.* Absolutely gorgeous.

On some level, somewhere, she had to believe there was a very good reason why he'd not worked harder on being involved with Rosie's life. Seeing him with his daughter now it seemed incredible that he hadn't.

'Is Wendy tired?'

'No. Well, not particularly. She's gone for a sleep now, but we finished early because we'd got to a sensible place to stop.'

In fact, they'd almost finished altogether. Did he know that? Wendy had already been more helpful than anyone had anticipated. One more visit would probably be all that was necessary—and then there'd be no reason to return here. She might never see Nick again. All of a sudden it seemed incredibly important that that shouldn't be allowed to happen.

Rosie tugged on her dress and signed for her to come with them. She pointed out into the garden and Lydia would have loved to simply nod. Instead she glanced uncertainly across at Nick, not even knowing whether he would have understood what his daughter was saying.

His expression looked slightly rueful. 'Would you like to join us?'

Lydia bit nervously on her lip. Did he want her to join them, or didn't he? Looking at him now, she couldn't see the faintest trace of the desire she'd seen earlier and all her lovely confidence faded.

As though he sensed her uncertainty, Nick added, 'We've got plenty of crisps.'

Lydia smiled and held tight on the young hand

in hers. It was all the encouragement she
needed. 'I'd love to join you.' She looked down
at Rosie and nodded. She was rewarded with a
sunny smile before Rosie shook free and tore
like lightning across the lawn.

'You'd think she'd be too hot to run like that,
wouldn't you?' Nick observed beside her.

She had to ask. 'Do you mind me joining
you?'

'Of course not.'

His reply was just a little too automatic. It
made her wonder what he'd have said if he
wasn't quite so 'British'. *What did he think of
her?* She really wanted to know. At least she did
if he'd revised his first impression of her. If
not…well, if not she probably didn't want to
know.

Lydia clipped her keys on to her belt. 'Do you
want me to carry anything?' she asked, looking
at the backpack, rolled up picnic rug and a
purple-coloured plastic box.

'No. I'm balanced.'

She nodded and turned to walk with him across
the lawn. It took an almost superhuman effort not

to ask him about Anastasia, or Ana as he called her. She wanted to know whether there was any possibility of Rosie living with her mother again or whether she was settled at Fenton Hall for good.

Instead she asked, 'Is it Rachel's day off? I haven't seen her today.'

He nodded. 'It's a college day.'

'But she's happy here?'

'So she says,' Nick replied. 'Rosie's ecstatic.'

Lydia nodded and wondered what to say next. She looked about her, taking in the formal rose garden near the house. 'Do you have a favourite picnic spot?'

'Not yet. This is a first for me.'

Of course he wouldn't have. Lydia watched her feet as they trod through the grass. He wouldn't have gone on a picnic because this was his first summer with his daughter. Seeing him with Rosie it was difficult to believe—and another thing she wanted to ask him about, but really mustn't.

'My preference today is for shade,' he said, looking down at her. 'How about you?'

'Shade's good.'

His smile twisted and then he asked, 'What was it you wanted to ask?'

Lydia gave a short laugh. 'How could you tell?'

He merely shook his head.

'Am I really that obvious?'

'To me.'

She looked away at the warm expression in his eyes. It scared her, but excited her too. The juxtaposition between the two extremes made it confusing. She hurried into speech without stopping to think whether it was wise or not. 'I was only thinking this must be your first summer with Rosie.'

'Apart from the summer she was born,' Nick agreed easily. 'She was nine months old when Ana left me.'

Anastasia Wilson had left *him*. That was a thought that was going to take a bit of getting used to. It didn't seem possible that any woman would prefer the overly bronzed playboy she now lived with over Nick.

But it was now or never. Lydia took a shallow breath. 'Anastasia Wilson. Wendy told me.'

'Did she?' His expression was inscrutable. It was really unnerving not to be able to tell what he was thinking, particularly when he seemed to be able to read her perfectly well.

'I—I asked her whether Rosie's mother had died.' She twisted round the gold bangle on her wrist.

'Ana?'

Lydia smiled. 'That's exactly what Wendy said. I'd not heard her referred to as anything other than "Ana", so I didn't know who she was.'

'Did Wendy tell you anything else?'

Lydia reviewed her options. She bit down on her lip. She could tell him Wendy's views on marriage, which he probably knew. Or that she hadn't liked his father, which, again, he probably knew. But that wasn't what he meant and she knew it. 'She said Anastasia isn't a natural mother.'

'That's true enough.'

Rosie skipped back and pointed at the ground before signing out the picnic mat.

'Over by the trees,' Nick said carefully,

pointing a short distance in front of them. Then he looked at Lydia. 'What's the sign for tree?'

Lydia made the sign, splaying her fingers. 'It's an obvious one. Use your hand to make the branches, your forearm is the trunk.'

'I think I can remember that one. It's more like charades.'

'Most signs are fairly straightforward. The knack is to think in pictures.'

'Such as?' They stopped at the base of a mature oak tree. Rosie was ready to help unpack everything. Nick laid a restraining hand on the top of her head. She looked up and he mouthed the word, 'Steady.'

He slipped the backpack off his back and set it on the ground. Rosie undid the buckle and struggled with the toggle which kept the top tightly closed. She looked up at Lydia, who stepped forward to open it.

Rosie reached in and pulled out a plastic box and unclipped the lid. Inside were tiny plastic Playmobile figures—a table, pram and assorted other things Lydia couldn't quite make out in the time they were held up to her.

Lydia turned round to find that Nick had spread out the picnic rug and sat down. 'Won't she lose the figures in the grass? Some of those pieces are very small.'

'I doubt it. She's incredibly dextrous and very careful. That box is part of an enormous plastic dolls' house she brought with her. She plays with it for hours. Far more than anything else.'

Lydia sat down on the rug and turned to watch Rosie as she set out tables and chairs among the tree roots and carefully balanced people in all the crevices. Quickly it began to take on the appearance of a little community and she moved her people around it, obviously lost in a world of her creating.

'It's amazing to watch,' Nick said. 'It's almost like she's directing an epic movie.'

Lydia turned back to look at him. 'It's very creative.'

'That's in her genes.' He pulled out a bottle of wine from an insulated bag and glanced at the label. 'Wine?'

She nodded.

Nick unscrewed the top and reached inside

the box for a flask of coffee. 'We're going to have to drink from the flask cups, but since you're the guest I'll let you have the one with the handle.'

He poured wine into the first cup and passed it over to her. 'It's Australian. I've no idea whether it's a good vintage or not, but I like it.'

Lydia accepted the plastic cup. 'I would have thought you'd be a wine connoisseur.'

'I'm reliably informed I have no palate,' he said, pouring some into the second cup. 'My father was passionate about his wines. He had a cellar built beneath our house which was kept at the optimum temperature. I thought it incredibly dull and cultivated a taste for everything he thought most contemptible.'

'As rebellions go that's fairly mild,' Lydia observed, taking a sip. 'This is nice. I wish I knew something about wines. I hear other people talking about it and they sound so educated.'

The lines to the sides of his eyes crinkled. She loved the way they did that. 'I'm sure you can make it sound like you know what you're talking about. This one is "crisp and refresh-ing"'. He held up the bottle. 'It says so on the label.'

Lydia smiled. 'I've got no palate either. My dad used to make his own wine. We used to have oil-fired central heating and there was a boiler house just behind the kitchen. Dad used to say it was the perfect place to ferment wine.'

'Was it good?'

'Terrible,' she said on a bubble of laughter. 'If I'm honest, it all tasted a little bit yeasty. The absolute worst was parsnip, although he made a potato wine which was pretty unpleasant…but drinkable with cheese.'

Nick's eyes glinted across at her and she felt a burst of sheer happiness. She could get used to this. Lazy summer days, picnics with wine, Nick…

She could get used to Nick.

The way his dark hair curled at the back of his neck. The way he focused his attention on you when you talked and made you feel important. She loved his slow laughter and the easy way he moved. Lydia watched as he unpacked the food from the picnic box and laid it in front of the rug. It was companionable. Easy. There were so few days in her life when she did something for no other reason than it gave her pleasure.

'Explain to me what you meant about thinking in pictures when you sign.'

'Well…' Lydia glanced over at Rosie, still playing in the shade of the tree. 'Rosie might prefer you to use sign support, which would mean you'd follow normal speech patterns, but BSL is different.'

'BSL being what the interpreters use in the bottom right of the television screen?'

Lydia nodded. 'British Sign Language. If you wanted to sign a story about a man standing on a bridge you need to build up a visual image with your signs. If you sign "man" first you've got him in a vacuum which doesn't mean much.'

'So?'

'You paint a picture. You start by signing "bridge" because that's where it all happens. If it's important where the bridge is you fill in what's around it. Maybe put in nearby trees…or a stream. A castle, if that's what's there.'

Nick smiled. 'I've got the sign for tree.'

'You place everything in your picture and only then do you bring in the man. He can be on the bridge or by the bridge, walking across the bridge or jumping off it. Everything is shown by where you place your fingers in the picture.'

'Sounds complicated.'

She shook her head. 'It isn't. It's actually quite logical.'

Nick watched the light play on the myriad tones in her hair. Streaks of gold, bronze, auburn and chestnut in a harmonious blend. Stunning. *She* was stunning.

He'd known, since that day in the kitchen garden, that he was attracted to her in a way he'd never been to anyone else. He'd thought he'd be able to control it if he didn't spend time with her, vanquish it. But he'd been wrong.

Nick watched as she unbuckled her sandal and slid her foot out to let her toes wiggle in the grass. She was unconsciously sexy. Ana struck poses, but Lydia simply was. Her long elegant fingers played with the gold chain at her neck and he saw the small pulse that beat there.

Avoiding her hadn't helped at all. Trying to keep away from her had only served to heighten his awareness of everything about her. She pushed her hair to one side and then twisted it round and pulled it through into a knot at the back of her head. Her movements were swift, practised…and sexy. Nick looked away, almost unable to cope with seeing the long graceful curve of her pale neck.

'It's hot.'

Nick glanced back. 'Don't you like the heat?'

'I'm the wrong colouring. Izzy and I both burn easily. Mum was a true redhead. We both missed out on the hair, but got the freckles.'

Nick looked closer and saw the fine dusting of freckles over her nose. Fresh, pale and beautiful.

Rosie brought over a small figure and held it out to Lydia, her hands flying as she told her something.

Lydia bent over the figure and then looked up. 'I can't do this.'

'What?' The vibrant colour of her eyes almost stopped him from breathing.

'The hat is stuck on too tightly.' She held it out and Nick reached across to take it.

He'd never believed it in movies when people seemed to imply a touch could be electric, but the merest touch of her fingers sent him into overdrive. Nick bent over the figure and pushed off the medieval headdress it wore, glad when the plastic moved. He looked up to see Rosie had settled comfortably in Lydia's lap.

Her beautiful hands lightly touched Rosie's arms and her head bent and softly kissed the top of his daughter's hair. Nick swallowed the lump that had settled in his throat.

He was falling in love with her.

Please, no. Never again.

If a miracle happened and Lydia could be persuaded to stay for him, it couldn't last. One day she'd wake up, just like Ana, and realise she was bored. There was no point pursuing something that couldn't have a future. Particularly since this time, he had the strongest feeling, he would never recover.

After a moment he held out the figure. 'Here.'

Rosie leapt up and quickly signed a thank you

before taking the figure. It was unbelievable to him that he could recognise the sign as easily as if she'd spoken to him.

And all that was because of Lydia. If she hadn't pricked his conscience he might still have been locked in a completely separate world from his daughter. It didn't bear thinking about.

'Rosie doesn't look like she burns,' Lydia remarked, her face turned away to watch as Rosie carefully clipped on a different hat before balancing the figure. 'I always wanted that kind of olive-tinted skin. I always thought it looked exotic.'

Nick had to turn away. Lydia had no idea what exotic was. Exotic was the vibrancy in her hair, the mystical depths of her eyes, the way the layers of her ethnic skirt swung about her long legs. It was the tiny Celtic toe-ring she wore and nails painted in an extravagant shade of copper.

'She doesn't seem to burn, but I ought to put some more cream on,' he said, settling on the prosaic.

Lydia swung back to look at him. 'So should I. I never do remember and then I suffer later.'

'Use ours.' Nick reached into the backpack and pulled out a bottle of sun protection. 'It's got a factor of forty.'

Lydia took the bottle and squeezed a little out into her hand; it shone green in her palm. 'Is it supposed to be that colour?'

He felt his mouth twitch. 'It's so you can see where you've applied it. It fades.'

'So if I put this on I'm going to be green?'

'In the short-term,' he agreed.

Lydia looked at him doubtfully, as though she knew how near he was to laughing. Gingerly she smeared green streaks up her arm. 'You're sure this fades?'

'It's a brilliant idea when you have a wriggling five-year-old.'

'I'm not five!'

No, she wasn't five. Nick watched as she gently smoothed the lotion up her arms, across her shoulders, up her neck.

Gingerly she dabbed a faint smear across her nose and blended it in. 'Have I missed anywhere?'

Nick moved closer and reached out to touch her face. His thumb moved lightly across her cheekbone. 'There's a little bit…' And then his voice dried up. He couldn't think what he'd been about to say. He only knew how it felt to be touching her. Really touching her.

Her eyes were wide, flecked gold and stunningly beautiful. He saw her lips part softly and heard her sharp intake of breath.

God held him. He felt as if he was being drawn in as surely as a fisherman brought in his catch. It was inevitable. No escape.

He'd been fooling himself thinking there was still time to save himself from hurt—*he already loved her.*

And he wanted to kiss her. Make love to her. He so desperately wanted to make love to her.

There was no choice any more. He would settle for whatever she could give him for as long as she could give it.

'You're so beautiful.' He murmured the words against her mouth as his lips closed against hers. His hand twisted in through the soft knot at the back of her head and dimly he was aware of the cascade of hair that fell like a curtain about her shoulders.

Her lips trembled beneath his as though she was uncertain and then she relaxed into him. And for one moment all he could think of was her and how incredible it felt to hold her.

CHAPTER NINE

ON SOME level Lydia had always known that Nick would kiss like that. Her heart hammered painfully against her chest and her skin tingled where his hand touched. She heard the soft guttural sound of triumph he made as he pulled her in closer and felt her own spirit soar in response.

Then he tensed. Lydia wanted to cry out in protest as he started to pull back…and then she remembered Rosie. Probably a fraction after he had.

Rosie.

Lydia looked across at Rosie, wondering how much she'd seen. Her dark head was bent over her game, her concentration totally focused on what she was doing. It seemed she'd seen nothing, but that could so easily not have been the case.

She cast a glance up at Nick. What had they been thinking of?

Nick's eyes travelled back from Rosie to her. 'I'm sorry.'

She shrugged, trying to convey an easy unconcern. It was just a kiss, she reminded herself, not a lifelong commitment. Lydia gathered her hair together in a long coil and twisted it back up.

Why had he said he was sorry? She didn't want him to be sorry. Sorry implied that he thought kissing her had been a mistake, and it hadn't felt like a mistake. It had felt…inevitable.

It was terrifying to look into his dark eyes and feel herself falling deeper and deeper into them. She'd never experienced anything quite like this in her entire life.

She was thirty years old, for crying out loud. She'd been in several reasonably serious relationships over the past ten years. She'd even, on two occasions, wondered whether she might have been in love. A simple kiss should have meant nothing, but this…intensity was outside her experience.

Lydia picked up her wine. It was the feeling of being out of control. Never before had she felt so vulnerable. This felt like walking out on a tightrope knowing the safety net had been removed.

When Nick looked at her he made her feel so many conflicting things at the same time. Part of her felt breathless and afraid, another part felt invincible, as though she could achieve anything.

And when she looked into his dark eyes she knew he wasn't sorry he'd kissed her, whatever he said to the contrary. She believed he hadn't intended to, any more than she'd intended to kiss him. But sorry? No, he wasn't sorry.

He'd pulled back only when he'd remembered Rosie. *As had she.* So now what?

'More wine?'

'I still have some.' Lydia put her cup down on the grass.

'Something to eat?'

Lydia accepted the plate Nick handed her and opened out a packet of crisps on to it. Every movement seemed as if it needed thought; even breathing had become unusually difficult.

She was aware when Nick looked at her. Equally aware when he looked away. And it was mutual, she was sure of it. The *frisson* between them crackled like a live thing.

Had Izzy felt like that about Steven Daly? The disquieting thought slid into her head with the same potency as the snake into the Garden of Eden.

It was a relief when Rosie noticed that the food had started to be unpacked and left her game to join them. Blissfully unaware of any undercurrents, Rosie concentrated on decimating a small fairy cake which had been filled with butter-cream.

Nick reached out and touched his daughter's hand, shaking his head when she looked up.

'Why do children do that?' Lydia asked, momentarily distracted by Rosie's uninhibited excavation of the butter-cream with her forefinger. 'I always used to eat the jam out of a jam tart first and Izzy used to lick the chocolate off a chocolate biscuit.' She reached out and took a large crisp and snapped it in half. 'I'd forgotten we used to do that. What was your childhood fetish?'

'I didn't have one.'

Lydia tucked her skirt around her legs. 'You must have.'

He shook his head before she'd finished speaking. 'I wasn't allowed any. My father paid for very expensive nannies whose primary role was to instil rigid discipline in me.'

Lydia gave silent thanks for her own childhood. There'd been times when she'd been ashamed of her parents, wished they'd not stood out from other parents—but she'd had no idea how lucky she'd been.

'That's sad,' she said, thinking of how much her parents had simply enjoyed Izzy and her. It made her ashamed she'd ever been ashamed. Grateful for the heritage she had without ever knowing she possessed it.

'The only subversive influence in my life is Wendy.'

Lydia looked up and smiled. 'She must have done her best.'

'Always.' His smile widened at some distant memory and then he said, 'I was never sure whether she involved herself in my life because she knew how much it annoyed my father or whether she really felt her role as my godmother was a sacred trust.'

Lydia picked at the grass beside her. 'Perhaps a bit of both,' she said, thinking back to her conversation with Wendy earlier. 'If your father didn't like her, why was she asked to be your godmother?'

'Money.'

'I'm sorry?' Lydia said, not quite sure she'd heard him correctly.

His eyes glinted with amusement. 'The expressed reason, given at the time, was that Wendy was my mother's second cousin. Wendy's conviction, however, is my father had an eye to her money.'

Lydia immediately thought of Wendy's cottage with its antiquated kitchen and tired decoration. *What money?* She'd thought Nick culpable for letting his godmother live in such a way. Even after she'd got to know Wendy better, understood her proud and indomitable spirit, she still thought he should have done something to help her. But if Wendy was rich…

Nick seemed to read her mind. 'Don't let the way she chooses to live fool you.'

'But—'

Rosie's knee knocked her plastic cup and sent orange juice spilling out across the rug. Lydia lifted her skirt out of the way and accepted the pieces of kitchen towel Nick passed her.

'Has she got you?'

Lydia shook her head. 'Just the rug and the boxes.' She lifted one box up and carefully wiped the plastic bottom. Nick, meanwhile, refilled Rosie's cup.

'Now sit down this time,' he said slowly, making sure his daughter was watching his mouth. 'Careful.'

Rosie wasn't in the slightest bit cowed. She smiled and curled up against him.

Lydia balled up the damp paper towels. 'Have you got a bag to put these in?' He reached behind him and produced a carrier bag and Lydia tossed them inside.

She then asked, 'Why does Wendy chose to live in…?' She waved her hand about rather than use the word which came to mind.

'Genteel decay?'

Lydia nodded.

'She likes it.'

'But… Why would she…?'

Nick took pity on her. 'I've tried to persuade her to make the cottage more comfortable, but it doesn't interest her. She maintains she has considerably more than most of the world population—'

'That's true, I suppose.'

'And she doesn't care whether her decoration is this year's fashion or last.'

Lydia could hear Wendy saying it. Her lips twitched and she couldn't resist saying, 'Or from the seventies.'

'You haven't seen the bedroom. It's back in the forties.' He took Rosie's cup from where she'd precariously placed it and settled it in the middle of the rug. 'Like the kitchen, which she tells me was cutting edge in its day.'

It seemed all her prejudices concerning Nick were falling like a pack of cards. *All her prejudices except one.* His daughter curled in even closer and rested her head on his lap.

'She's tired,' Lydia observed.

Nick lightly stroked her curls. 'I suppose it's hot and she's been running about most of the morning.'

Lydia longed to ask him about Rosie. Why had he had so little say over her upbringing, so little contact with her prior to her coming to live with him? She almost blurted out a question, but stopped short. One kiss didn't seem to give her the right to ask.

She watched the rhythmic movement of his fingers through Rosie's curls and the sleepy way her dark fringed eyelids closed. 'She's going to sleep.'

His hand didn't stop and gradually Rosie's breathing slowed and her thumb found its way into her mouth. Lydia looked up at Nick. The love on his face squeezed her heart.

'Has it been difficult organising your work so you can be with Rosie?' Lydia asked softly.

'Very.' Nick's fingers stilled, but stayed buried deep in Rosie's riot of curls. It looked almost like a benediction. 'I did it because it seemed like the right thing to do.'

Lydia nodded. She imagined Nick would be good on duty, which was why she found it so incredible he hadn't maintained some kind of contact with his daughter even when his ex-wife had custody.

'I've been surprised at how effective I can be from home…and just how few days I've needed to be in London. Long term I'll need to be there more than I've been there over the past couple of weeks, but I've learnt a lot about balance.'

Balance. She'd heard colleagues talk about a life/work balance, but it was a concept that was completely alien to her. For her, there was only work. It was her driving passion. The phone would ring, day or night, and she was ready to go.

She'd missed weddings, surprise parties, planned parties, even the presentation of her then-boyfriend's OBE. She never accepted any invitation without adding the proviso that she might be called away. Nothing had ever got in the way of work.

Except, perhaps, Izzy's overdose.

That event had sent a ripple through her life

strong enough to send her off course—for a time. But there hadn't been any major conflict of interest. Nothing she'd had any difficulty in refusing, and before long she'd been on the trail of Steven Daly's insurance scam.

'The biggest surprise—' and Lydia could hear it in his voice '—is how much I've enjoyed it. I used to be on the motorway into London at around six and I'd never be home before seven on a normal working day. But being with Rosie…' he shook his head as though he couldn't quite believe it '—is incredible. I don't want to miss any more time with her than I have to.'

Lydia felt the same pang of envy she'd experienced watching them from the window. Seeing Nick, his hand buried in Rosie's rampant curls, she felt she was missing out on something important.

'What about you?' Nick asked. 'What's your five-year plan?'

Lydia pleated the fine flame-coloured cotton of her skirt. It was an interesting question because she didn't have a plan. She'd never had

a plan and wasn't sure how to answer. She
hadn't thought about doing anything different,
within the next five years or beyond. She'd
always go where there were stories to tell. It
was her life. It defined who she was.

But why? She'd never thought about the why.
Or even what she'd do if she allowed for the possibility of change.

'My plan,' she said slowly, 'is to go with the
opportunities. On some level, I suppose, I still
want to change the world.'

'And have a garden again one day?'

'Perhaps.' Lydia twisted the bangle at her
wrist. 'It would be nice to think I will one day,
but it's not very likely. I'm away from home far
too much to make it practical.'

He nodded as though he understood what she
was saying, had even expected it. She hated
thinking he somehow thought less of her because
of it. Why was it you had to sacrifice so much of
one part of your life to make another part
possible?

Would she, in the same position, have made
the same choice Nick had?

She suddenly understood what it really meant not to have made any space in her life for the possibility of children—ever. It was a huge decision which, surely, warranted more thought than she'd given it? Was she really going to live her entire life without any emotional commitments?

At the core of every relationship she'd ever had was the knowledge that they would never hold each other back in their dreams. She'd absolutely bought one hundred per cent into the idea that relationships were secondary to careers.

She could honestly say she'd happily sent the men in her life off to report on war zones and to take photographs of Namibia—whatever had been their particular passion—without a qualm. And she'd demanded the same in return. It was what happened in mature twenty-first century relationships.

But...

Those relationships had floundered. The careers had pulled hard and eventually there had been nothing left to come back to. Ten years and there'd never been any sense of her being the centre of anyone's universe. She'd never been the dream.

And she'd never found anyone who could be hers. Maybe she was more like Anastasia Wilson than she cared to think.

'Will Rosie's mother see much of her?' Lydia asked.

'I doubt it. She'll come occasionally, probably bringing presents, but—' his voice took on a possessive quality '—day-to-day, no.'

'What did she say about Sophie leaving?'

Nick looked up. 'Nothing.'

'Nothing?'

'Her mind was completely taken up by the late delivery of some silk.' And then, as he saw her face, 'Ana never wanted to be a mother. I always knew she would have preferred not to have to juggle her career with raising a child.'

'But—'

'Rosie wasn't a planned pregnancy.' Nick looked down at his little girl. He should have fought harder for a relationship with her. Other fathers did. He knew of men who drove hundreds of miles to see their children every other weekend.

Nick looked up at Lydia, watching her wide eyes for some glimmer of what she was thinking. He blamed himself. Did she blame him?

'When Ana left…' He cleared his throat, his hand moving against Rosie's curls. 'Ana left when Rosie was nine months old…'

'I know. You told me,' Lydia said softly.

It would be easy to stop there, tell her nothing more—but he wanted her to understand. There *had* been mitigating circumstances and he wanted Lydia to know them.

'Ana left me for my best friend.'

There was some satisfaction in seeing her mouth part in shock.

His voice lowered. It was still difficult to put words on what had happened. 'Gaston Girard. I'd known him since we were seven. His mother had married an Englishman and we went to the same boarding school…until tennis took over his life. But we remained friends.'

Lydia shook her head, part sympathy, part disbelief. 'Nick, I'm…so sorry.'

'It lasted a year.' Nick swallowed. 'Slightly over. Gaston was on the international tennis circuit then. I tried to make trips to see Rosie, but it was…difficult and she was only a baby. With long gaps in between visits I could have been anyone.'

He stopped speaking and Lydia leaned forward to touch him. Her fingers lightly brushed his forearm and Nick risked looking across into her eyes. So beautiful, they shone with unshed tears.

'I'm so sorry. If I'd known…I would never have… It must have been so….'

Impossible. It had been impossible. For months he'd steeled himself to make those visits; each one had been harder than the last, until he'd found reasons why he couldn't go.

The sense of betrayal had been so acute. Seeing Gaston… Just seeing the three of them together…

Nick swallowed painfully as he remembered how it had felt to see his best friend with Ana. Taking his place with Rosie. It had killed him.

Each visit had been harder than the last. Every

time he'd seen it the reality had sunk in just that little bit deeper. It had been easier to pretend it wasn't really happening. He'd poured himself into his business. Had tried to blot it out.

'I tried again when Ana left Gaston and returned to England—'

Lydia's beautiful eyes never left his face.

'—but by then Rosie was two and hid behind Georgina's skirt. Georgina was Ana's mother,' he clarified.

Lydia nodded.

'After three or four times like that I stopped visiting regularly. I sent money, presents… The usual kind of things people do which means they don't have to invest too much of themselves.'

The hand on his arm tightened and he risked looking directly into Lydia's stunning eyes.

Some part of him had braced himself for rejection, but all he saw was a compassionate understanding. 'You have her now,' she said softly.

'Yes, I do.'

Unbelievably. Back then, when Ana had decided to leave with Gaston, that had seemed an impossibility. But he did. He had Rosie. He would be the 'father' she remembered and the person who had the privilege of guiding her future.

It was the nearest he'd come to forgiving himself. He'd refused to talk about that time, but telling Lydia...seeing her reaction...had been cathartic.

In his lap Rosie stirred. Her young body uncurled like a bud and she sat up, her eyes sleepy.

Above her head Nick met Lydia's eyes. 'We'd better get back. It's late.'

'Yes.' Lydia's response had been automatic, but she glanced down at her watch. It *was* late.

It was time for her to head home, but that seemed even less appealing now than it had earlier. Her flat would be empty. Quiet.

How had Nick endured that time? She ached for him. Couldn't think of what to say—other than to apologise for her own self-righteous attitude towards him. She hadn't had all the facts. She'd had no right to judge...

Lydia stood up and shook the crumbs off her

skirt. She looked up and caught Rosie watching her, her face curious. Lydia smiled and signed that it was time to pack up and go home.

Rosie nodded happily and then walked over to slip her young hand trustingly inside Lydia's. She led her towards her make-believe world at the foot of the tree and Lydia looked down at the intricate family groups. It seemed a shame to break it up and, for some reason, it made her feel tearful.

Carefully she helped Rosie fit the figures back in the box. She raked the ground so as not to leave behind a single piece, while behind her she could hear Nick packing up their picnic.

How could she have been so sanctimonious? Why had he allowed her to lecture him on his responsibilities as a parent?

She'd wanted to know why he hadn't learnt to sign for Rosie—and now she knew. But she hadn't expected how painful it would be to hear it. She knew the law was biased in favour of mothers, would probably have campaigned for just that bias, but… Nick had lost so much. That didn't seem fair.

They headed back towards the house. Rosie's short sleep seemed to have given her all the refreshment of a full eight hours. She scampered ahead, occasionally turning round to smile at them and check they were within sight.

Lydia glanced across at Nick and wondered what kind of relationship she could hope to have with him. Her tentative smile faltered. One kiss and she was imagining all kinds of possibilities.

Illogical.

Wasn't it?

Except it wasn't—and she knew it. She glanced down at her feet and watched the way her nails shone through the grass. There was something in his dark eyes that told her he would contact her when he was in London. They'd have dinner…

What then?

How much of a difference did it make if your boyfriend had a child? From what she'd observed from friends, they didn't usually introduce their children to their girlfriends until the relationship had reached the stage of a duplicate set of toiletries and at least one drawer in the bedroom. But they'd begun the wrong way up. She already knew she loved Rosie.

Love. Had she really thought that? Did she love Rosie? Lydia cast a surreptitious glance up at Nick. And what about Rosie's father? How did she feel about him? Just thinking about the possibility of loving him, being in love with him, turned her insides to marshmallow.

And it scared her. Love shouldn't feel like that, should it? Lydia frowned. What was she frightened of? And then she knew. *Love meant sacrifice.* Putting another person before you and trusting they were looking out for you.

She didn't do that. Ever. And Nick needed that. Listening to him talk about losing Rosie had made her realise that.

'How much longer will you be meeting up with Wendy?'

'We're practically finished,' Lydia answered, watching Rosie run down a bank, arms spread wide. 'I'll be here again on Thursday.'

'Thursday?'

She looked across at him and nodded. 'I've got

a couple of articles to deliver for next week and a launch party to go to for Caitlin Kelsey's *Beyond Redemption*.'

Any moment he was going to ask her to dinner. She could feel it in the air. It was as real as the smell of summer carried on the gentle breeze. He'd arrange to meet in London. They'd have dinner and afterwards...

Her imagination was full of images. In an ideal world she'd simply have said 'yes'. She wanted nothing more than to know what he looked like in the morning, to wake with his arms wrapped around her. She wanted to surprise the laughter that transformed his face.

But Nick wasn't looking for the 'see you when we're in the same city' kind of relationship she favoured. He was too responsible to bring a steady stream of girlfriends through Rosie's life. He needed the sort of woman who would fit into country living and be a fantastic stepmother to Rosie.

If she could wave a magic wand and change her personality she'd do it. If she could be the kind of woman who got emotional satisfaction from a lemon-fresh toilet and a freshly baked tray of cupcakes…

If…

As he turned to look at her she heard her own small intake of breath as she took in the expression in his eyes. It was timeless. Unmistakable. *She wasn't ready for this. Didn't know what she thought yet.*

But even as the panic ripped through her she felt time slow down around her. Slowly, deliberately, his eyes moved to her lips and she knew he was going to kiss her.

For the second time.

Her breath seemed to catch in her throat. She wanted to feel his lips on hers. Coaxing a response. Making her forget that this wasn't a good idea. That she wasn't the woman…

The small distance between them vanished. *Dear God.* His mouth was warm and persuasive on hers. She could taste the wine and the strength that was entirely him.

For one brief moment she tried to be sensible. She pulled away and murmured, 'Rosie. We…'

His hands moved to cradle her face, his eyes

seeming to read her soul. 'Knows the way home.'

Nick moved slowly, deliberately. He gave her every opportunity to pull away, decide this wasn't what she wanted, but Lydia found she couldn't resist any more.

Her hands pushed the backpack off his shoulders and she heard it hit the grass. She heard her own soft moan of pleasure as his mouth trailed up the side of her neck, the small whimper that begged for more.

'Nick.' His name on a breath.

Her mind refused to co-operate. She couldn't formulate the words, didn't really know what she wanted to say. He nipped softly at her earlobe and her head fell back, a mute invitation which she couldn't stop and didn't want to.

There was only the sensation of him and a slow warmth spreading through her body. His tongue flicked between her parted lips, coaxing a need in her she hadn't known she was capable of feeling.

His hands moved over her body and pulled her in closer…and then closer. Lydia could feel his arousal hard against her stomach and the soft answering ache settling low in her abdomen.

She wasn't strong enough to walk away from this. She wanted him. As perhaps she'd never wanted anything. She wanted him to push the straps of her sundress down, wanted to be naked before him. She wanted him full and moving within her…

She'd never felt like this. So completely abandoned, so…

'We'd better go inside,' Nick murmured, his breath ragged. His lips moved against her neck.

'Yes.' More groan than anything else.

And deep down Lydia knew she was saying 'yes' to more than walking inside Fenton Hall.

Lydia stretched languorously, her body warm and sated. She felt completely…new, as though this were the start of something wonderful. Unexpected, but completely wonderful. She rolled over on to one side and looked at Nick's sleeping face.

She'd wanted to know what he looked like in the morning. And he looked wonderful. The early morning sunlight worked its way through the partly opened curtain and shimmered against his bare shoulders. Lydia reached out and stroked along his collar-bone and down the smooth skin of his back. It was irresistible. He was irresistible.

Nick's eyes opened, his voice low and gravelly. 'Good morning.'

This ought to feel embarrassing, some part of her brain registered. She'd never…well, she had, but she'd never spent the night with a man she wasn't in a long-term, seriously thought about relationship with. But Nick…

Nick had been so sudden. Cataclysmic. Absolutely nothing she'd ever felt about him had been neutral, not since the first time she'd seen him.

That seemed a lifetime ago now. Standing on the roof of his godmother's cottage, with him so angry and disapproving below. They'd moved such a long way towards each other.

She let her fingers splay out on his back, loving the warmth of his skin. 'Morning.' Her voice sounded breathless.

Then he smiled, that slow unexpected smile that had always made her melt. 'I can't believe you're here.' He rolled over and imprisoned her beneath him. His hands pushed back her hair.

'I can't believe I'm here either. I don't—'

Nick bent his head and kissed the spot on her neck he'd discovered last night sent her wild and she let her hands curl into his thick hair.

'Don't what?' Lydia heard the teasing laughter in his voice. 'Are you sorry?'

That was an easier question to answer. 'No.' *Not sorry at all.* Her whole body was singing with remembered pleasure. Her limbs felt heavy and it was purgatory to think of moving.

He kissed her, a slow drugging kiss that made it even harder to say, 'But I do need to go home, Nick.'

In an ideal world they would have a lazy breakfast, the opportunity to make love some more, have lunch…

His eyes gleamed with passion. Nick bent his head and kissed her again. She loved the way he kissed her. She loved being with him. She loved…

Being loved. He'd not said the words, but that was how he made her feel. When he touched her she felt worshipped. His arms wrapped around her and she felt completely protected from all life's traumas. She'd never be sorry.

'Stay.'

That one word sent a spiral of desire coursing through her body. There was nothing she'd like more than to stay. She lifted a finger and traced it along his now roughened jawline. 'What's the point in our creeping around the house last night if I'm still here when Rosie wakes up this morning?'

Nick grunted and rolled off her. He laid back, one arm bent behind his head, his eyes glinting sinfully and his body completely relaxed. 'I hate it that you're right.'

Lydia gave a low husky laugh and flung back the bedclothes. She picked up her sundress and looked around for her bra. 'Where…' she began before she noticed that Nick was openly watching her. 'Stop it!'

His smile stretched as Lydia held her dress up in front of her. It was too late for modesty, way too late. And strange, that after everything they'd shared, she should still feel shy.

'Rosie is your daughter,' she said with mock severity. 'It's five o'clock and time I was gone. What time does she wake up?'

Reluctantly Nick pushed back the covers. 'Six.' He bent down and picked up his jeans and flung them across the bed.

Lydia stood like some nervous virgin, envying how at ease he was with his body. So much for the British inhibition she'd thought an integral part of him. Total confidence. A man completely at ease within his own skin.

He flung a silk dressing gown around his lean body. 'When will I see you again?' he asked, taking her face between his hands and kissing her gently. It was the kind of kiss that gave comfort, made her feel incredibly special. He pulled back and looked into her eyes. 'Make it soon.'

Lydia felt her shyness recede. She reached out and touched his face, his stubble rough against her hand. 'Come to London.'

CHAPTER TEN

LYDIA knew it was work the minute she looked at her mobile. The call hadn't been entirely unexpected. There'd been rumours that she might be given this particular opportunity because of her interest in politics and human rights. The recent journalistic award hadn't done her any harm either.

Brussels.

She was going to Brussels.

But the way she felt about it was entirely unexpected. She kept hearing Nick's words—'time away from Rosie is time wasted'. She hadn't really understood what he'd meant, but she did now. Time away from Nick felt like time wasted.

Lydia lifted her hands to her burning cheeks. She didn't want to go. For the first time in nearly ten years she didn't want to go. Seven nights and five days of Nick spread over three weeks and she didn't want to go.

It should have been everything she'd ever wanted. The chance to report on real issues that would affect Europe for the next decade and beyond. But a year…

Minimum. A year was a long time.

Lydia pulled a chair up against her wardrobe and stood on it to lift down her suitcase. She could still see Nick. She was being ridiculous. True enough long-distance relationships rarely worked, but that would be his choice. She could fly back to see him every few weeks. Perhaps he'd even find the time to come over and see her.

And Rosie. She'd be an excellent role model for Rosie. It would be good for her to grow up seeing women achieving things, being their own person.

Brussels. The European Parliament.

This was everything she'd ever wanted. She was going to be at the centre of things. It was what she'd been working for.

So why did she want to cry?

Lydia slowly opened her wardrobe and started laying out the clothes she'd need to take. A pair of well-cut black trousers, two brown. Two sharply cut jackets and a simple cream evening dress. She placed them in a pile on the bed.

It was just the thought of going. Once she was on the plane she'd be fine. Excited.

Of course she'd be excited. It was a completely fantastic opportunity. She was going to be at the hub of Europe, getting to talk to the people who were making the decisions.

Lydia put the first few things in her suitcase. This was what she'd wanted. Always. From the age of eighteen she'd wanted the excitement of change. She'd wanted the kind of career that meant a phone call could see her flying to a disaster area in Scotland and then the Olympics next. She wanted adventure. Variety.

She wanted the respect of other journalists. She still wanted to change the world, be a force for good and the champion of the underdog.

Always. It was her lifelong goal. It was why she'd left Izzy crying in Auntie Margaret's small back bedroom and caught the coach to

Cambridge all those years ago. It was why she'd pushed herself to get a first—because anything else wasn't going to be good enough to justify what she'd done to her sister.

Lydia sat down on the edge of her bed. So what had changed? If she didn't pursue her goal now it meant she'd let Izzy down for nothing.

The temperature outside was soaring, but inside she felt so cold. She felt as if she was being ripped in half, as though she was being forcibly torn away from what was really important.

How she was feeling made no sense. She'd always avoided emotional ties. Had never put down roots. She'd made sure she had no responsibilities, no children and no relationships she couldn't leave. It was different for her male colleagues. For them it was possible to truly 'have it all', but she'd accepted long ago that men rarely followed their partners around the world.

It was a simple choice. And she'd made it. At eighteen. She'd always known what she wanted. She'd never needed to put together a five-year plan—she had a mission statement.

It was *who* she was.

She was a career journalist, one hundred per cent committed to what she was doing. So why did she feel so...broken. No, not broken, more sick inside. Deep down, heart-wrenchingly sick.

Lydia pulled her Anastasia Wilson jacket from the wardrobe. Her hand hesitated as she put it in her suitcase, her fingers resting on the soft leather. She'd not asked Nick about why his marriage had failed. It hadn't seemed...appropriate to talk about his ex-wife and he hadn't volunteered the information.

It was another of those unwritten twenty-first century rules—never talk about past relationships. If they were over, then they were in the past and best forgotten.

How ridiculous. The ending of a marriage had to be something that shaped you, coloured the way you thought about your future. She hadn't wanted a post mortem on it, but it would have been useful to have known why. Perhaps Nick had found it difficult to be with a woman who couldn't put him first?

And Rosie, that inner voice whispered, she didn't need another career woman in her life.

She needed a different kind of role model. She needed someone who would be there for her, loving her.

Lydia put in the last of her things and zipped her case shut. She couldn't be that person. Nick had to have known that.

By tonight she would be on the plane to Brussels. She would be fully focused on the opportunities and challenges ahead of her. It would be fine.

She glanced round her bedroom. One suitcase was probably everything she'd need for now. She could come back and collect anything else she wanted when she'd arranged an apartment.

There was just time to see Nick. She lifted her case and carried it out to the lift. It would be better to see him face to face. Explain. Say goodbye to Rosie. Then she could drive to Wendy's cottage and spend an hour or so with her before driving on to the airport. She'd have to leave the car in the long-stay car park for the time being, but all that could be sorted out later.

Her mind started to turn over the thousands of ways she could tell Nick she was moving to

Brussels, but the journey to Fenton Hall wasn't quite long enough to fix on the perfect one. Confronted with him she made a mess of it.

His face, usually so inscrutable, showed surprise. 'You're leaving tonight?'

She nodded. 'Late afternoon. So I'm going to have to take a rain check on dinner.'

'Of course.'

Nick tried to look as though he was excited for her. She was obviously buzzing with it, loving the opportunity she'd been given—and he could see it was a good one. Lydia would enjoy being in Brussels and she was just the kind of journalist who needed to be there. She was passionate about what she did—and that was great.

It just didn't feel great.

And he'd only himself to blame. He'd known that what he'd found with her could only be temporary. That sooner or later she'd be off, chasing another story, searching out another wrong that needed to be righted.

He loved that about her. There was precious little he didn't love about her.

'I'll be back in a couple of weeks. Obviously

I'll need to get my things,' Lydia said brightly. 'But there's no point dragging everything out at this stage.'

'What time is your plane?' He forced himself to ask the question. He was doing well.

'Four.'

He made rapid calculations. How long it took to drive to the airport, how long before she had to be there before she boarded her flight. *How long before she left him.*

'I'm packed and ready to go. I promised Wendy I'd stop by her cottage today. She's got some letters she wants me to have.'

Lydia was going now. Nick felt as if he needed to shout, hit something, walk for miles…

Instead he smiled. 'You need to get going.'

She nodded. 'I just stopped by to tell you I'm off and…to say I'll phone.' She smiled.

Nick felt as if his heart had been ripped out and stamped on. He loved her—and he was going to have to let her go because that was what she wanted. And he was going to let her go without guilt.

He'd known exactly what he was getting

himself into. In the beginning, when he'd first met Lydia, he'd thought she was like Ana—but that wasn't the case. It had taken him a while to understand that.

Ana used anything and everything to build her career. She'd married him because he had the money she'd needed to bolster her fledgling business. She'd left him for Gaston because he could introduce her into the international jet-set world she wanted to be part of. With Simon Cameron she'd finally joined the establishment.

Lydia was completely different. She believed passionately in what she was doing. She truly believed she could change the world—and who was he to say she couldn't?

It was what Wendy had seen in her from the very beginning. The reason why she'd insisted on Lydia as her biographer. His godmother shared the same burning desire to make her life count and she'd achieved so much. He admired her. He admired Lydia.

He loved the way she gave herself passionately to whatever she was doing and if he'd hoped he might become her passion then that had been entirely at his own risk. He'd known that from the moment he'd realised that avoiding her wasn't going to make the pain of living without her any less intense.

He turned as he heard Rosie's feet scurry down the hall. Lydia bent down so she could lip-read clearly, her hands moving in confirmation. Nick watched his daughter's face change. She was free to express what he couldn't.

Her hands flew, her movements were jerky. He hadn't learnt enough to understand what she was saying, but he got the gist from the expression on her face.

'I've got to go to work,' Lydia said, pulling her close and holding her.

Nick reached out and touched Rosie's shoulder. His daughter looked up at him, her brown eyes questioning. He nodded in confirmation of what Lydia had said. 'We'll see her soon.'

Then he looked at Lydia. Her excitement had faded and her face looked pinched. Maybe she wasn't finding this as easy as it had first appeared? Maybe she would find she wanted to come back to them? To him. But he had to let her go first. It had to be her choice.

Which meant he had to say goodbye—with Rosie looking on. It was up there among the hardest things he'd ever had to do in his entire life. 'I'll miss you.'

'I'll ring.'

He nodded. *He'd never told her he loved her.* It had never seemed quite the right moment. He'd wondered whether it was too soon, whether it would put undue pressure on her. At least that was what he'd told himself. The truth was he'd been scared it would drive her away.

But she was going anyway. He should have told her. It would have made no difference to what was happening now, but he would have said the words.

Rosie pulled away and ran back down the hallway, her feet echoing on the wooden floor. 'What?'

'She said to wait.' He watched as Lydia took her lip between her teeth. She gave a gasping breath. 'This is so hard.'

'Lydia, I—'

She tried to smile and her mouth wavered. 'I'm sorry. I didn't think it would be this difficult…' She swiped at her eyes.

Nick just needed to hold her. He drew her in close and let his hand snake up to cradle her head. Her hair was soft against his arm and smelt of roses. *He loved her.* More than that, he ached for her.

For a moment they just stood there. 'I do have to go,' she murmured softly, her voice choked.

'I know.' Nick pulled back and looked into her incredible eyes. 'I know you do.'

Lydia reached out and touched his face and then she leant forward to kiss him. He knew exactly what her trembling lips were saying—it was thank you.

He felt the tremor pass through his body. She hadn't left yet and he felt utterly bereft. He would see her again. Brussels wasn't the end of the earth—but she knew and he knew she'd made the choice to walk away from them. It would never be the same.

They heard Rosie's footsteps coming down the stairs and Lydia instinctively stepped back.

Every impulse prompted him to snatch her back into his arms, but he resisted. Instead he looked down at his daughter. 'What have you got?'

Her young face was very solemn as she held out a white envelope on which she'd carefully drawn a stamp in the top right-hand corner. Lydia took it. 'What is it?'

Rosie made a single sign.

Lydia bent down. 'Oh, honey, I'll remember you.' She made the sign. 'I'll remember you and I'll see you both soon.'

Then she stood up and left, without daring to look back at them. Nick watched her car snake down the drive until it had completely disappeared—and, in that moment, he knew how it felt to die.

If Wendy noticed she'd been crying she didn't say anything. She accepted Lydia's help in carrying the tea through to her small lounge and settled herself in the armchair.

'Brussels?'

Lydia nodded, trying to instil some kind of excitement into her voice. 'For a year.'

'What a marvellous opportunity.' Wendy's eyes seemed unusually observant but she didn't say anything more. She sipped her tea and then appeared to change the subject.

'Pass me those letters.' Lydia stood up and walked over to the sideboard she'd pointed at. 'I thought you might like these. When I'm dead they'll only be thrown away and you might find them interesting background reading for the chapter on the Sudan.'

'Thank you.'

Wendy sat back in her chair. 'I wrote them to Nick's mother and I was very glad when George gave them back to me after she'd died. She was a wonderful correspondent, kept me in touch with what was going on at home. It can be very lonely saving the world.' Her mouth twisted in a smile. 'It's not for everyone, Lydia, my kind of life.'

Lydia looked up. She knew enough of Wendy to know she never spoke without an agenda. Often she spoke to stir up debate, but sometimes…sometimes she spoke because she wanted to be listened to.

'There are days now when I wonder whether I made the right choice. You know, people are more important than anything. More important than causes. I think I lost sight of that a little.'

Wendy paused to sip her tea. 'You have to know what kind of person you are. I prefer humanity when it's at a distance. I'm better at loving "people" as a whole than trying to love any one individual. But that comes at a cost.'

Her sharp blue eyes looked over the top of her teacup. 'Do you understand what I mean?'

Lydia nodded. She wasn't sure that she did.

'This is how I've chosen to live.' She looked round her dark sitting room. 'It suits who I am. I like not being answerable to any other person, but…I have chosen to be alone.'

There was a small silence and Wendy stretched out her hand. 'It's not my business to tell you how to live your life, but don't shut out other possibilities and other ways of being useful.

'Sharing your life with someone doesn't mean you can't make a difference. In many ways you can make more of a difference.'

Lydia felt the tears well up behind her eyes. She wasn't sure what to say. 'Nick… I—'

Wendy sat back in her chair. 'I don't need to know, but if you think I didn't suspect something was going on between you two you must think I hurt more than my ankle.'

Amidst the pain Lydia felt a bubble of laughter. 'I don't, I—'

'And, to tell you the truth, I envied you. I could have married, had a family of my own, but—' she shook her head '—I was never brave enough to risk my happiness on another person.

'I just want you to think about it. It might be right for you to live a life like mine. Maybe the causes you have will be enough for you. When you're my age and you look back on what you've achieved…what is it you'd like people to say about you? What is it you'd like to have done?'

What was it she'd like to have done? Lydia thought about it all the way to the airport. She thought about it as she boarded the plane and as she landed in Brussels. She thought about it as she checked into her hotel.

She cared about so many things. Justice. She cared passionately about justice. About fairness. About the starving. About the poor and oppressed. About the environment. About social deprivation.

They were the big issues—and in a way it was easier to care about them. There was distance in that. Lydia sat down on her hotel bed. She understood what Wendy had been saying about preferring humanity as a whole rather than individuals.

She had never thought about it before. Caring for individuals was more painful. Loving them was a risk. The things that had hurt her most had all been about individuals, when she thought about it.

University had been an easy focus to deflect her from grieving. She'd masked the pain of her parents' death by campaigning for 'big' causes. Her need for a career had had nothing to do with Izzy. She saw that now. Her sister wouldn't want that of her.

As an adult Izzy had told her she was glad she'd let her grow up with her cousins and not tried to hold it together alone. She hadn't blamed her for not rescuing her from Steven Daly. All that guilt she'd placed on herself.

Why had it taken until now for her to be able to see it?

She'd spent years hiding from her emotions. Her career had been a convenient focus. A shield.

When her parents had died...

When Izzy had taken her overdose...

Those were the events that had changed her life. Had altered her. Loving people came at a personal cost. When she thought about the people she loved or had loved she thought of her parents, Izzy, Rosie...

She wanted Rosie's life to be wonderful. She wanted to make sure her childhood was as perfect as it could be, that she grew up feeling loved and cared for. She wanted to make sure there was proper provision for her at school and that she wasn't stuck at the back of a class, only seeing a teacher for the deaf once a week.

She was passionate about that? *Was it wrong to care about that more than some international disaster?*

And she loved Nick.

Nick.

She loved him. Lydia looked at the cream-painted walls of a hotel room that could have been in any city in any country of the world. *What was she doing here?*

Did she really want a life like Wendy's? Wendy Bennington, human rights campaigner, acclaimed by many, but at the end of each day she was alone. Did she really want that?

Lydia lifted her handbag on to the bed and pulled out the envelope Rosie had given her.

The stamp she'd drawn in the corner showed a sad face and squiggles to indicate the perforations. *It had given Nick time to kiss her.*

Her fingers shook slightly as she tore open the top. Inside was a drawing and a photograph. The photograph was of Nick and her. Lydia smiled and ran her fingers over his face. It was one Rosie had taken. The image wasn't central and she was slightly out of focus, but it was nice to have a photograph of Nick.

Lydia stood up and walked over to the kettle and propped the photograph inside the picture frame on the wall. Then she opened out the drawing.

Rosie had drawn a house with a sun in the corner of the picture. She'd coloured the roof in red and the door in green. It was a picture any clever five-year-old might have drawn, but in the foreground she'd drawn three people. One much smaller than the others and all three were holding hands.

Lydia felt as if someone had reached in and squeezed her heart until it cried blood. Rosie had drawn a family. *Them?* She'd said she'd drawn it so that Lydia would remember.

Then she glanced back at the photo—and at Nick's face. He was looking down at her, the expression in his face one of total love and acceptance.

How had she missed that? She felt the first tears start to fall as she reached for the telephone. She'd never been so unsure as to what she should do.

Her sister's voice sounded sleepy.

'Izzy, it's Lydia. I need to talk to you…'

Nick kissed Rosie goodbye and waved her off with Rachel. His life had taken on a strange pattern over the past few days. He felt list-less. Lost.

No prizes for guessing why that was. Lydia hadn't phoned. She'd be busy sorting out her life in Brussels. He knew that. He had her mobile number and he could have rung it any time, but the thought of hearing her voice and not being able to hold her was torture.

He stood at the window and watched the rain come down in stair-rods. Was it raining where Lydia was? Was she happy? Missing him?

Thinking about him at all?

Then he saw her car. It was almost as though he'd conjured her up by thinking about her. He left the sitting room and went out into the hallway, almost not believing she was real.

Christine stopped him. 'Lydia Stanford asked for the gates to be opened. I've let her through.'

Nick didn't wait for his housekeeper to finish speaking. He walked out of the front door and stood foolishly in the rain, his face, hair, T-shirt quickly becoming soaked through.

Lydia saw him.

She sat for a moment clutching Rosie's

picture. She'd come so many hundreds of miles and she didn't know what to say. She might be about to make a complete and utter fool of herself. She wasn't sure she could do it.

What if she'd misread Nick's expression in the photograph? What if she'd been a momentary diversion? What if…?

She looked up. Nick was waiting. He must be wondering what she was doing letting him get soaking wet. Slowly she opened the car door and climbed out. The rain poured down on her, but she scarcely noticed. Nick didn't move towards her, didn't say anything. He was watching, waiting.

'I couldn't do it,' she managed, her voice broken. She held up Rosie's drawing, now completely sodden but the wax picture still there. 'I opened Rosie's envelope and I couldn't do it. Brussels. I've told them I can't do it. That I needed to come…' *Home.*

She was crying, but her face was so wet with rainwater it couldn't matter. If he didn't speak soon she was going to wish the ground would open up and swallow her whole.

She tried again. 'It's a family…' Her voice broke. '*Nick.* She drew a family. She drew us.'

Please understand, she begged silently. She'd never felt so vulnerable as she did now. She had meant to tell him that she loved him, but she was too frightened to say the words.

Help me.

And then he moved, slowly.

His hands cradled her face and he reached down to kiss her. He must have known she was crying then because she could taste the salt in her own tears.

She was wet, cold, tired and…happy. Her hands snaked round him and held him close. He felt so reassuringly solid. Real. And he hadn't rejected her. He didn't seem to blame her for leaving.

Then he pulled her away and stared down into her eyes. 'I love you.'

She felt as if the floor had disappeared beneath her feet. Was it really going to be that simple? 'Why didn't you ask me to stay?'

'Would you have?'

'I might have done.' Then she thought. 'Probably. I think. I don't know.'

His mouth twisted. 'I nearly did, but I forced myself to let you go. I thought that was what you wanted. I don't want to be a compromise on the life you really want.'

'You're not.' And that was the moment Lydia knew Wendy had been right. She had a new passion, one that transcended every other passion. It didn't take away from the other things she could or would do with her life, it would only add to it. 'I love you.'

Nick put his arm round her and led her into the house. They dripped on the beautiful wooden floor.

'I must look a mess.'

'You look beautiful.' His words echoed what he'd said before and she smiled.

'I'm sorry, Nick.'

He gathered her close and she could hear his heart beating and feel the soft kiss he placed on her hair.

'I'm so sorry I had to go away to realise how much I love you.'

He tilted her face and kissed her. Then he smiled, that heart-stopping beautiful smile that made her bones turn to liquid, and carefully interwove his fingers through hers. 'I didn't want to hold you back. You've got such dreams and I...I didn't want you to ever feel you'd sacrificed too much.'

'But if it's what I choose...'

Nick lifted her up in his arms and carried her up the wide staircase as though she weighed nothing. 'If it's what you choose, then that's completely different—and I'll support you absolutely with whatever you want to do in the future.'

'Ditto.'

He set her down inside his bedroom. 'You're soaking; let me help you.' He reached out to peel away her wet top, but stopped to kiss her. 'Marry me?'

Lydia smiled. 'I've got every intention of marrying you, but not if you propose to me while you're taking my clothes off! I'm not telling my grandchildren that.'

Nick smiled that smile as he pulled her in closer. His voice was warm against her ear. 'Then lie.'

MILLS & BOON® PUBLISH EIGHT LARGE PRINT TITLES A MONTH. THESE ARE THE EIGHT TITLES FOR AUGUST 2006

❧

THE BILLIONAIRE BOSS'S FORBIDDEN MISTRESS
Miranda Lee

MILLION-DOLLAR LOVE-CHILD
Sarah Morgan

THE ITALIAN'S FORCED BRIDE
Kate Walker

THE GREEK'S BRIDAL PURCHASE
Susan Stephens

MEANT-TO-BE MARRIAGE
Rebecca Winters

THE FIVE-YEAR BABY SECRET
Liz Fielding

BLUE MOON BRIDE
Renee Roszel

MILLIONAIRE DAD: WIFE NEEDED
Natasha Oakley

MILLS & BOON®

Live the emotion

0706 Rom LP

MILLS & BOON® PUBLISH EIGHT LARGE PRINT TITLES A MONTH. THESE ARE THE EIGHT TITLES FOR SEPTEMBER 2006

THE GREEK'S CHOSEN WIFE
Lynne Graham

JACK RIORDAN'S BABY
Anne Mather

THE SHEIKH'S DISOBEDIENT BRIDE
Jane Porter

WIFE AGAINST HER WILL
Sara Craven

THE CATTLE BARON'S BRIDE
Margaret Way

THE CINDERELLA FACTOR
Sophie Weston

CLAIMING HIS FAMILY
Barbara Hannay

WIFE AND MOTHER WANTED
Nicola Marsh

MILLS & BOON®

Live the emotion

0806 Rom LP